JACI BURTON

ELLORA'S CAVE
ROMANTICA PUBLISHING

An Ellora's Cave Romantica Publication

www.ellorascave.com

Fall Fury

ISBN 1843609665, 9781419951220
ALL RIGHTS RESERVED.
Fall Fury Copyright © 2004 Jaci Burton
Edited by Briana St. James.
Cover art by Syneca.

This book printed in the U.S.A. by Jasmine–Jade Enterprises, LLC.

Trade paperback Publication June 2004

Content Advisory:

S – ENSUOUS
E – ROTIC
X – TREME

Ellora's Cave Publishing offers three levels of Romantica™ reading entertainment: S (S-ensuous), E (E-rotic), and X (X-treme).

The following material contains graphic sexual content meant for mature readers. This story has been rated E–rotic.

S-*ensuous* love scenes are explicit and leave nothing to the imagination.

E-*rotic* love scenes are explicit, leave nothing to the imagination, and are high in volume per the overall word count. E-rated titles might contain material that some readers find objectionable—in other words, almost anything goes, sexually. E-rated titles are the most graphic titles we carry in terms of both sexual language and descriptiveness in these works of literature.

X-*treme* titles differ from E-rated titles only in plot premise and storyline execution. Stories designated with the letter X tend to contain difficult or controversial subject matter not for the faint of heart.

Also by Jaci Burton

ಐ

About the Author

ℬ

Jaci Burton has been a dreamer and lover of romance her entire life. Consumed with stories of passion, love and happily ever afters, she finally pulled her fantasy characters out of her head and put them on paper. Writing allows her to showcase the rainbow of emotions that result from falling in love.

Jaci lives in Oklahoma with her husband (her fiercest writing critic and sexy inspiration), stepdaughter and three wild and crazy dogs. Her sons are grown and live on opposite coasts and don't bother her nearly as often as she'd like them to. When she isn't writing stories of passion and romance, she can usually be found at the gym, reading a great book, or working on her computer, trying to figure out how she can pull more than twenty-four hours out of a single day.

Jaci welcomes comments from readers. You can find her website and email address on her author bio page at www.ellorascave.com.

Tell Us What You Think

We appreciate hearing reader opinions about our books. You can email us at Comments@EllorasCave.com.

FALL FURY
Devlin Dynasty 2

જી

Dedication

∽

To my wonderful editor, Briana St. James, and to the
publishers of Ellora's Cave, for letting me write the
stories that live in my heart, no matter what. I am forever
grateful that you allow my imagination to run free.

To Mel, Patti, Missy and Ani…who loved Max and
Shannon's story as much as I did. Thank you for telling
me I wasn't crazy. Love and hugs to you all!

And to Charlie, my alpha male. The one who makes my
blood run hot, my pulse race and my heart soar with a
magic I had never known existed until we met. I love you.

Prologue
Early September
Boston, Massachusetts

႙

Max Devlin heaved a sigh and opened the doors to his father's library.

They were all in the room, gathered together for another family meeting. He already knew the subject, knew what was going to be discussed, and how it would affect him.

His parents smiled at him, and he smiled back, already feeling the strange sense of loss, even though it would be another few weeks before he left. Family was everything. The pack wasn't supposed to separate. But what James and Patricia Devlin ordered was law. As his parents and the prime leaders of their pack, no one would second guess their plans for the future. He knew it was as hard for them to let go as it was for all of them to leave. They hadn't made the decision lightly, but the future of their kind rested on the Devlins and other families like theirs.

"Hey everyone," he said, forcing a smile that he didn't feel.

Jason looked up and grinned, then put his arm around Kelsey, his fiancée. She smiled tentatively, still feeling her way around the Devlin brood. She wasn't shy, which was a good thing with this family. But he sensed a hesitance about her, almost as if she wasn't yet sure whether or not they'd all pounce on her at any given moment. Max smiled at the thought.

"Hi Max," she said.

He stopped and kissed her cheek. "Settling in okay?"

She nodded. "Yes. Surprisingly. I thought it would be…"

"Weirder?" he offered in response.

Kelsey laughed, her face lighting up. It was easy to see why Jason had fallen in love with her. "Yes, that's a good enough word."

"Let me tell you a secret. We *are* weird. Get used to it."

"I'll keep that in mind." She turned and winked at Jason, who grinned like an idiot. Max shook his head. What was it about men after they fell in love? They became giddy morons. Thank God he'd managed to escape so far.

But he knew his days were numbered. He just hoped when it happened he wouldn't look as stupid as Jason did right now. Lovesick puppy was an understatement.

His younger brothers were there, too, currently shooting pool in the corner of the room. Conner and Noah nodded and resumed playing their game.

"Where's Chantal?"

"Upstairs on the phone," his mother said, rolling her eyes. "That girl is all business. She never seems to relax."

Max laughed. "Chantal's just driven, like the rest of us."

"More so than the rest of us," Jason added. "I'm always trying to get her to come to D.C. and visit, but she claims to be 'busy'."

"Would you all knock off the 'we're worried about Chantal' song and dance? I'm fine."

Max turned and grinned at his sister as she entered the room. "It's because you're the baby of the family, Chantal. You know how we like to protect you."

Chantal rolled her eyes, her raven hair pulled back, not a hair out of place as always. Even in blue jeans and a T-shirt, she emitted class. She rolled her eyes at Max. "Puleez. I'm hardly a baby."

A fact that wasn't lost on any of her older brothers, which is what kicked in their tendency to overprotect her. With Max nearly ready to depart for New Orleans, he'd worry even more.

"Quit obsessing over your sister," his mother said. "She's perfectly capable of taking care of herself. She is, after all, a successful lawyer."

"Shark is more like it," Conner mumbled as he bent over the pool table.

"Screw you, Conner. I'm no more shark than you," Chantal replied, sticking her tongue out at her brother.

"Welcome to the family, Kelsey," Max said as he walked by her on his way to the bar. "Are you sure you know what you've gotten yourself into?"

Kelsey grinned and leaned her head against Jason's chest. "Yes, I think I do. You all love each other, you just show it by fighting."

"Like a snarling pack of wolves?" he offered.

Chantal snorted and Conner and Noah grinned.

"Something along those lines, yes," Kelsey said, knowledge glimmering in her eyes. She knew, and she accepted. He wondered if he'd end up as lucky as Jason had.

"Okay, let's get serious," his father said. "Jason obviously already has a stronghold in the nation's capitol. Max, how are plans going for your move to New Orleans?"

With all their busy schedules, they hadn't had a full family meeting in a long time. Since Jason had brought Kelsey up for the weekend, his parents had called for one. "Plans are right on target. Just wrapping up some loose ends at the office. I'll be out of here by the end of the month, ready to meet with the Storm family about their public relations program."

"Good. And you know what else needs to be done."

Like it hadn't been drummed into his head for the past six months. "I've got it covered, Dad."

"Good. Chantal, have you looked into the San Francisco connections yet?"

"Yes, Dad. I'm working on it. So far it looks like I have a job lined up with one of the firms in the financial district there."

"Excellent. Now it's just a matter of deciding on a location for Conner and Noah."

Max watched his brothers' faces as they looked up from the pool table toward their father. Like all of them, they knew they'd go wherever their parents sent them. The hard part was not knowing where and when.

Good thing they were all independent sorts, capable of managing out there on their own.

Eventually they'd all be leaving, because that was their destiny. The Devlins had big plans. Plans that would take them nationwide and eventually worldwide. Max felt at least a little comfort in knowing they'd soon all be in the same boat.

"I'll miss you, even though you're a huge pain," Chantal said, approaching him at the bar.

He fixed a drink for her and handed it to her, then kissed her on the cheek. "I'll miss you too, little monster. Who will I pick on after I leave here?"

She laughed and threw her arms around him for a hug. "You'll find someone. I'm sure of that."

He already had, but it was too early to mention anything to his family. Later, after he confirmed whether his instincts were right or not, he'd let them know. Right now he needed to concentrate on getting his life in order for his move to the south.

To the land of hell.

Max downed his whiskey in one gulp, dreading the coming trip, but knowing his future was no longer in Boston.

It was in Louisiana, with Shannon Storm.

Chapter One
Late September
Louisiana

෨

Max read the road sign looming ahead with a sense of finality.

Welcome to Louisiana.

Louisiana. Nothing like Boston. The pavement ahead shimmered, glowing with an unnatural wave of heat. It appeared as if he were driving right into another dimension.

Pretty damn close to it, at least in his mind.

Interstate Ten led all the way into New Orleans. He turned down the thermostat to cool things off as the heat pressed down on him. Maybe the shimmering waves of hell outside had found a way into his SUV. What was up with the weather here? It was late September, but felt like mid-July. The heat was stifling, making him wish he'd worn shorts and a tank top instead of jeans and a tight-fitting polo shirt.

And he had to move here. Permanently. Sometimes he wondered if the Devlin clan had a touch of insanity running through them.

He shook his head, the voices of his parents lingering in his mind. *Branch out into the southern territories. Find and locate packs already established in the area, if there are any. Take over. And while you're at it, find a mate and start a new business.*

Easy for them to say. They got to stay in Boston while they sent their children to strange places to start new.

His older brother, Jason, had succeeded in Washington, D.C. Not only was he a successful politician, but he'd also just landed himself a mate. He'd brought Kelsey up to Boston to meet them not more than two weeks ago. She was beautiful and obviously head over heels in love with Jason. And despite being human, she'd readily accepted their family and their...idiosyncrasies.

Now it was his turn, and he'd have to find his fate in New Orleans, of all places.

What a bunch of bullshit. Why couldn't one of his brothers have come down here instead? Yeah, yeah, yeah. He already knew the answer. This was his destiny, or some other such bullshit spouted by his mother and father. Sometimes that just sucked as an explanation, especially when faced with having to move to hell.

Max loved Boston. Everything about it. Not only were his people there, but all that was familiar. Friends, bars, places to hang out. Seasons, even. Snow. Leaves changing color in the fall. Damn, Louisiana was probably this hot in January. And they didn't even have a professional baseball team. Well, not a major league team, anyway. And anything lower than the majors just wasn't baseball, in his opinion. First thing he was going to do when he bought a house was have satellite installed. He'd die without his Red Sox.

Before that happened, though, he'd have to get things set up at The Rising Storm, the hotel of the Storm family, his latest and greatest public relations venture. He'd had several conversations with Logan Storm about their new casino venture. His friend and fellow Bostonian, Melissa Cross, had fallen madly in love with one of the Storms and was in the process of making a permanent move.

At least he'd know one person in this humid abyss.

He cranked up the stereo, the driving beat helping to keep him awake after the long trip. He wanted a shower, preferably a cold one, and then a nice, soft bed to catch a few hours shuteye.

Then he'd have to meet with the Storm family. He knew from conversations with Logan that he'd be working with their sister, Shannon, head of The Rising Storm's Public Relations Department. He'd heard of her, knew what kind of businesswoman she was. He'd even read articles about her PR style and what a go-getter she was.

They called her a tiger in a business suit. From the pictures he'd seen of her in magazines, he wondered what else she growled over.

The last article he'd read was in the Louisiana Business Magazine. All about how she single-handedly increased exposure for the Storm family holdings in New Orleans.

He remembered the full-page picture of her in that article. She'd been dressed in a pale blue suit, her dark hair pulled tightly away from her face. And what a striking face it was.

From the first moment he'd seen her picture, her image had remained burned in his mind. Turquoise eyes sparkled with intelligence. A cool exterior masked an elemental warmth underneath. Her hair picked up the light of the camera, reminding him of a wolf's coat. Was it long or short? It shined a luxurious sable in the glossy magazine picture. Would it be as soft to the touch?

His cock stirred, the all-too familiar ache settling between his legs, making him yearn for someone to rule beside him.

Too much time for business lately and not nearly enough time to play. He was thirty years old, well past the age to find a life mate. That anxious, nervous feeling seemed to permeate his being every full moon. He found himself wandering far too often lately, that sense of searching, but not finding, nearly overpowering him, leaving him unfulfilled for the first time in his life.

He needed a woman. He might not like the idea, but there was no avoiding it. And he hadn't been able to find one, not "the" one. When an alpha found his mate, he damn well knew it. But out of all the women he'd been with, no one had given him that spark.

One woman had, and what sparked him had been nothing more than a photograph. But why her instead of women he'd met in the flesh?

There were plenty of women in Boston, all shapes and sizes. Some like him, others completely human. He'd had a lot of them, too. Many would have killed to become his life mate.

The only thing he'd gotten from any of them had been a momentary relief from the lust that seemed to grow ever stronger inside him with each passing year. Once temporarily satiated, though, he always lost interest.

His kind required a strong alpha female. He'd yet to find one, despite the primal urge that called to him

He was tired of feeling empty, no matter how busy his days and nights. It was time for a mate.

Time to meet Shannon Storm and see if she compelled him in person, as much as she had on the page of a magazine.

That would happen soon enough, and if Max was anything, he was a patient man. Tonight he might want to prowl. A familiar restlessness settled over him, no doubt due to two days traveling in this box on wheels. He needed to stretch out and go for a run, acquaint himself with the sounds and scents of New Orleans. And maybe, just maybe, find out if other packs currently controlled southeast Louisiana.

His agenda was full already. Time to prioritize. Job, pack search, and mate.

Although how he was supposed to transform when it was ninety-eight goddamn degrees in September, was beyond him. Yeah, Boston summers were hot, but this was nothing like what he was used to. The air outside just sucked the oxygen right from his lungs.

New Orleans—one helluva place to take up residence.

* * * * *

16

Shannon Storm paced her office, her heels clicking on the smooth surface of the gleaming wood floors.

"Would you stop that? You're making me dizzy."

She halted mid-stride and turned to Melissa Cross, her soon-to-be sister-in-law. Shrugging, she said, "Sorry, Lissa. I'm thinking."

Melissa crossed her legs and tugged at her navy skirt. "So I see. Thinking about what?"

How could she explain that she couldn't describe her feelings? They made no sense to her. Trying to tell someone else what rolled through her mind would be impossible. She felt…restless. And excited. Like a child anticipating Christmas morning and what awaited her. But as hard as she tried to pinpoint some event, she had no clue what excited her.

It was fall. Her season. Yet summer lingered on, as if trying to keep her at bay. Though she tried not to buy into the magic that was a part of her, she also was pragmatic enough to acknowledge it existed. The season of fall was when she was most comfortable with her power, almost as if it were an annual unleashing of all the pent-up anxieties she controlled throughout the year.

But this year there was a delay in fall, and the humid stickiness just added to her irritation. That had to be the reason she felt the way she did. What else could there be?

Work was normal, the hotel/casino project moving along, and the PR plan in place. She was going to meet Max Devlin, the hotshot PR guy Melissa had recommended, and he was going to work on the plan with her.

"You're pissy about Max coming to help out, aren't you?" Melissa asked.

Funny how Lissa could nearly read her mind after only knowing her a few months. "I'm not pissy. I'm irritated. I can run public relations just fine on my own. I don't need some Yankee coming down here and trying to tell me how to do my job."

Lissa coughed and covered her mouth, but Shannon caught the smile she tried to hide. Feigning a serious expression, Lissa said, "I'm sure he won't do that. Granted, he's a shark in business, but I think you'll be impressed once you meet him."

She didn't want to meet him. She didn't want to have to deal with any interference on this project. "I'll deal with him because Logan consulted him without my approval and invited him down here. Otherwise, I'd kick his ass all the way back to Boston."

"I'd sell tickets to that event."

She offered a mock glare. "Smartass. And I used to think you were so nice."

"Oh, you love me and you know it."

Shannon smiled, pushing her annoyance to the back of her mind. "Yes, I do. You and Aidan haven't even gotten married yet and you're already my sister. By the way, where is your fiancé?"

"Meeting with Logan and going over some budget numbers for the marketing and PR plan."

Shannon scrunched her nose. "Ugh. I'm glad I'm not in on that meeting. I can only imagine how Mister-icy-calm-Logan will try to cram his budget numbers under Mister-hot-and-frenzied-Aidan. Although it would be fun to be a fly on the wall."

The sounds of male voices raised in anger sailed down the hallway of the Storm corporate offices. "I don't think we need to be a fly on the wall. They're both coming through loud and clear," Lissa offered, a sly smile gracing her face.

Shannon laughed. Her brothers were all voice, all talk, but deep down they had an abiding love and respect for each other that no one could tear down.

Lissa stood and looked at her watch. "I need to go. Are we still meeting Max when he gets in?"

"Yes. We're meeting in the conference room about six."

"Okay, that leaves me an hour or so, then. I expect the explosion between Aidan and Logan will be over soon. I should go back to my office and prepare myself for Aidan's arrival, followed by his venting tirade about how unreasonable Logan is."

"You poor baby. But you're the one who fell in love with the idiot. Now you have to deal with him."

With a wink, Melissa opened the door and said, "I love dealing with him. Besides, how can I resist a man who makes my body thunder, my orgasms strike like lightning and brings on rain in our bedroom?"

"TMI, sister," Shannon replied with a wink. Melissa laughed and closed the door behind her, leaving Shannon with the wild array of thoughts racing through her mind.

During that hour before she had to meet Max Devlin, she planned her strategy on how to gain the upper hand with him right away. He may be the wizard of the northeast in public relations, but she was no slouch herself. And he was in *her* *t*erritory now. He'd learn very quickly that he'd be taking a supporting role in their PR launch. If he had suggestions, she might listen. Might. Then again, she might not. After all, it hadn't been her idea to bring him down here. And while she might have promised Logan she'd work with Devlin, she didn't promise that she'd work with him as an equal partner.

He'd soon discover who was the alpha dog in this relationship. Besides, she'd have her family standing with her, so she had nothing to worry about.

Confident, she stepped out of her office and headed to the conference room, intent on arriving early and grabbing a prominent place at the table. After all, appearances were everything, as was preparation.

She swung through the oak double doors and stopped short.

The room wasn't empty. A man was in there, his back to her as he gazed out the tall windows behind the table. His dark suit had to have cost a fortune, and must have been custom-made, considering the way it hugged his body. His jet-black hair waved over the white starched collar of his shirt. A bit too long for what was considered professional, but damn if it wasn't sexy as hell as it curled in tiny wisps against his tanned neck.

He turned to her and something within her sparked an immediate recognition, as if her body knew him. Ridiculous, since they'd never met, but the chemical reaction was overpowering. She grabbed for the back of the nearest chair, her legs suddenly trembling. For some reason, her limbs wouldn't move.

She'd never had this kind of a response to a man before. Never.

Without speaking, he approached her. He didn't smile either, just walked toward her slowly, in a stealthy, sexy way that had her thinking things she shouldn't.

Thoughts like primal. Animal. Lust. Passion. Sex. Hot, sweaty, incredible sex.

His eyes were breathtaking, a combination of green and gold that melted together like an artist's palette. Lashes as dark as his hair swept up along his brows. His nose was narrow, his jaw square, his lips delectably full—the guy looked more like one of today's hot movie stars than just a regular man. That sensual mouth of his curved into a lethal smile, and she forced herself to meet his eyes, all the while curious as to why she had suddenly forgotten rudimentary biological functions—like breathing.

"Shannon Storm," he said, his voice as seductive as his appearance. "I'm Max Devlin."

He extended his hand, but for an instant she was afraid to make bodily contact with him, unsure if she could withhold her magical reaction to the maelstrom stirring inside her. As it was, she felt unsteady, her entire world shaken. And all she'd done was look at him.

The professional in her wouldn't stand for any of this teenage girl drooling over a man. She held out her hand, tucked the magic deep inside her and directed her thoughts away from sex and onto business. "Max. Welcome to The Rising Storm."

When he took her hand, her toes curled right inside her shoes. She sucked in her lower lip and fought the panic assailing her. Heat shot through every limb, every organ, settling somewhere between her legs. She moistened instantly, her nipples hardening and pressing against her thin, lacy bra.

Max's hand stilled. He closed his eyes for the briefest of seconds, then inhaled sharply. When he opened his eyes, he graced her with a smile so predatory it caused her pulse to leap.

No. She did *not* have physical reactions like this. She was losing control. When she tried to pull her hand away, he held on, as if he sensed her reluctance.

Unfortunately, his heated grip on her only served to bring forth the response she feared most. Irritation grew within her, mixed with an inexplicable lust that permeated every part of her body. Railing against the loss of control, she let loose a little of the magic boiling inside her. The heavy doors blew open as a fierce wind blew through the conference room, whipping tendrils of her hair from its tight chignon and nearly propelling her against his chest.

Fighting to control the magic, she gripped his hand and squeezed with all her might, hoping her power would zap him with a shot of electricity that would shoot him straight across the room. No man had ever been able to stand up to the ferocity of the elements once she unleashed them.

They stood surrounded by what could easily be classified as hurricane force winds, and yet Max wasn't even struggling for balance. His eyes had darkened, the green nearly obliterated by the golden hue that seemed to glow. His grip held firm to her, almost as if he had accepted her unspoken challenge to back off and decided that he wasn't going to budge.

Why wasn't he shocked? Why wasn't he running for his life? For God's sake, wind like this didn't occur within an office complex. He was supposed to be afraid, or at least show some concern about what the hell was going on.

Instead, he held onto her as if they had engaged in a battle of wills, and he was determined to come out the victor.

Over her dead body.

It would be inappropriate to present arcing lightning in the Storm corporate offices, but she sure felt like blowing out the floor-to-ceiling windows in the conference room right now. How dare he provoke her this way?!

This first meeting wasn't going at all the way she had planned.

So much for gaining the upper hand.

* * * * *

Max held tight to Shannon's hand, ignoring the wind rushing around him.

He was mesmerized by the stray sable hairs that had come loose, whipping against her face. But she didn't budge, just kept trying to pull her hand free.

Damn, she was gorgeous. More so than in the pictures he'd seen. Her tan suit complemented her skin, and a creamy silk blouse underneath the jacket ruffled in the gusts she'd created, revealing the upper swell of her breasts.

He was having a difficult time keeping his burgeoning erection from poking right through his suit. Thankfully, his jacket covered the evidence.

This woman was a power to be reckoned with. She had magic, that was obvious, because the gale force winds smacking him in the face right now sure as hell hadn't come from him. He felt the magic course through her, had felt it from the moment she'd walked through the doorway, as if whatever secrets she held inside magnetized him, telling him more about her than a normal man would ever know.

A normal human male, anyway. He wasn't human and his powers certainly weren't normal.

Shannon was beautiful, strong, obviously capable and really pissed off right now. He had to admire the fact that she wasn't the slightest bit afraid to show her anger. A clear attempt at establishing who was in charge here. Shannon was a perfect alpha female.

No doubt about it, he wanted her. Never before had a woman captured his interest so quickly. Her intense gaze fixed on his and held, her anger evident in the way her eyes narrowed, turning a tempestuous blue.

Max heard voices outside the conference room. Immediately, the wind died and he released her hand, then brushed his hair back and straightened his jacket. Shannon's face burned a bright red, her irritation still evident.

"What was that?" he asked, although he suspected he already knew the answer.

"Problems with the air conditioning system. Blows a major gasket every now and then and it's like a wind tunnel in here. I'll alert the maintenance staff."

Good recovery, which meant she could think on her feet. She quickly turned away, smoothed her hair into place and smiled when a group of people came in.

"Are we late, or are you early?" A tall man approached, hand outstretched.

"You must be Logan. I'm Max Devlin, and yes, I'm early. You're right on time."

"I see you've already met my sister, Shannon."

"Indeed I have," Max said. Shannon nodded and offered a tight smile. Max wanted to laugh at her discomfort, but also knew that making a good impression on the Storms was paramount to a successful launch of his New Orleans business.

A lovely woman with hair the color of raven's wings stepped up. Shorter than Shannon, her smile was filled with a welcoming warmth. "We're so glad you arrived safely, Max. I'm Kaitlyn Storm."

Her hand slipped gently inside his and he felt her quiet, calm strength. This one was much less volatile than her sister. "A pleasure, Kaitlyn."

Max spotted Melissa Cross, who walked in with a tall man by her side. That had to be Aidan Storm, her fiancé. She shook his hand and said, "Welcome to New Orleans, Max. Nice to have another of the Boston contingent here."

"And I'm Aidan Storm, Lissa's better half."

Max laughed. "Well, you're a pretty formidable group."

Logan nodded. "So we've been told. But no one here bites. Although Shannon has been known to chew up and spit out a few people in her time."

"Logan!" Shannon said, casting a vehement glare in her brother's direction.

A very tight family. And a powerful one, too. Max's senses went into overdrive as he picked up on the magic contained within each of the Storm siblings. It seemed that they each held control over the elements of nature. Heat, ice, wind, rain, lightning, all of it very potent. No wonder his blood had fired to life when he was offered the chance to work with them. His sixth sense told him there was something special about the Storm family. He'd just had no idea what it was until he actually stood in a room with them.

Good thing he wasn't easily intimidated. A weaker man would cower under such superior strength of will.

But he wasn't weak. Nor was he interested in establishing dominance over any of the Storms.

Except for Shannon. He and Shannon had a connection, one that she was obviously uncomfortable with. Good. Keeping her off balance was a start. Tilting her world completely upside down would come later. Right now, business was his number one priority.

Tea and water were brought in, and they all chatted amiably. The get-to-know-you part of any business venture.

"Have you had a chance to look over the campaign?" Logan asked.

"Yes. You have some great ideas and a really good start on a dynamite public relations program." He looked to Shannon, who lifted a brow as if she hadn't expected the compliment.

"Shannon's good at her job," Kaitlyn said. "She's run some amazing programs for the hotel as a whole, along with taking separate functions, such as my events planning, and promoting them throughout the southern states."

Melissa turned to him and grinned. "Shannon's PR program for the hotel/casino venture is very good."

He'd just bet it was. "Glad to hear that. I'll make it better."

"That's a pretty arrogant statement," Aidan said, crossing his arms.

Max knew this was coming. "Yes, it is. But I back up what I say with results. No offense to Shannon at all. You've made a great start. Now it's time to refine it, improve it, and take it out there across the country. Whatever your PR plan was for Louisiana and the surrounding states, I'll improve it so that you can promote nationally."

Shannon tapped her pencil against the dark wood of the table, the annoying cadence the only sound in the room. It was as if her family was poised and waiting for the explosion they knew was coming.

Max expected it. Hell, he welcomed it.

Finally, she looked at him, her eyes as cool as he wished the weather was. "I think you're full of shit. There's not a damn thing wrong with The Rising Storm's public relations campaign."

"Afraid of a little constructive criticism? Concerned that I might come up with a better idea?"

"I'm not afraid, nor am I concerned. I simply think you have your head up your ass and haven't done your research."

"What if I've done thorough research and still think I can improve your plan? Are you so conceited about your work that you wouldn't even take a look at what I have to offer?"

Her eyes widened, then shot icy daggers across the table at him. Max remained relaxed, enjoying a battle more than anything. This was positioning of the alphas. Her against him. And he intended to come out the winner. It was just a matter of time before Shannon realized that. However, since she didn't yet know about him, he'd give her a little time to adjust before he attacked.

She looked around the table at her siblings, then shrugged. "You're here, although I didn't ask for you. I'll take a look at what you have."

He tried to prevent the grin of pure satisfaction that threatened to break out on his face, but had one hell of a time masking the triumph he felt.

Logan stood and smiled at Max. "Well, damn fine job passing the Storm test. We're not an easy bunch and speak our mind."

"I'll take an honest gut reaction over a load of bullshit any day. I don't mind a little battle every now and then. Keeps the blood moving."

Logan grinned. "You'll do just fine here."

Shannon snorted and mumbled something about arrogant assholes under her breath. She assumed he couldn't hear, but then again, she didn't know about his ultra keen senses.

The rest of them said their goodbyes, agreeing to meet later in the week after he'd had a chance to go over the plan with Shannon.

She started to walk out, but he wanted some time alone with her, and didn't want to wait. "Shannon."

She stopped, her shoulders tensing. Good, he wanted her riled up a bit. He liked her that way. She turned, arching a brow. "There's more? I thought for sure you'd shot your entire wad of insults about my work in one conversation."

"I didn't insult your work; I just said it could stand some improvements."

"You're an arrogant bastard, aren't you?"

He smiled. "So I've been told."

"On a regular basis, I assume?"

Damn she was a fireball. Just the kind of mate he needed, the kind of woman he'd want to rule beside him. Strong, capable, take no prisoners. "More often than not, yeah. But I didn't get to the position I'm in now without pissing a few people off in the process."

"You've done a fine job for your first day. I'll talk to you in the morning."

"Have dinner with me."

She opened her mouth and he knew the word "no" was going to come sailing out. But then she surprised him by asking, "Why?"

"Because I don't want you to think I'm a prick all the time." Which was true. He wanted her to know he was in charge, but not a prick.

The corners of her mouth lifted in a slight smile. "Don't shatter my illusions of you, Max. I prefer thinking you're a prick all the time."

"Well, I love to prove people wrong. Have dinner with me. I just got into town and have no idea where to eat. You wouldn't want me to sample the wrong Cajun food, would you?"

She rolled her eyes and glanced at her watch. "I'm busy."

"You have to eat."

"I already have a mother. Don't need another one."

"Where's that southern hospitality I keep hearing about?"

She let out a disgusted sigh. Ah yes, he knew that would get her. She looked him up and down, regarding him as if she wasn't sure she could trust him.

If she were smart, she'd run like hell, because he sure wasn't trustworthy where she was concerned. No way could he keep his hands to himself.

"Fine. Give me an hour to wrap things up and I'll meet you in the lobby."

Max admired the slight sway to her hips as she turned and walked out. Subtle, but definitely there. Her legs were long and shapely, and he'd wager a guess she was either a runner or a tennis player. Good. She could run with the pack easily then.

After he converted her, after he claimed her as his.

His balls tightened, his cock springing to life at the thought of making Shannon Storm his mate.

Whether she liked it or not, they shared a destiny. He was patient in some areas, not in others. Considering he was already primed and ready for sex, his patience was going to run out quickly where she was concerned.

Time to put his plan into action.

Chapter Two

ᔮ

Shannon paced the lobby and waited for Max, annoyed at herself for so readily agreeing to go out to dinner with him.

As if she wanted to spend time with the overbearing, conceited Yankee, anyway, let alone outside the normal business day.

She spotted him exiting the elevator at the other end of the lobby. He stopped to speak to Logan as he passed by the door to the corporate offices.

"He's hot, isn't he?"

She turned to see Kaitlyn peering around her. "He's okay."

Kaitlyn stepped in front of her, her amber eyes widening. "Then you're blind, *soeur douce*. He is perfection. Has to be a couple inches over six foot tall, wide shoulders, narrow hips, broad chest. And those eyes. I swear I've never seen eyes such a mesmerizing color."

"Like I said. He's okay." And that was all she'd admit to, otherwise she'd be bound and gagged and headed to the altar within twenty-four hours. Kaitlyn was as much a matchmaker as their mother.

"He's more than okay. And clearly he's attracted to you."

Shannon crossed her arms and turned her attention toward her sister and away from Max. "Oh right. Insulting me in the first ten minutes of our meeting was a definite clue that he has the hots for me."

"He's an aggressive alpha male, Shan. You know the type. God knows we've dated plenty. Most are assholes. Max isn't like that, I can tell already."

"Uh huh. What was your first clue? His incredible charm, or the way he slammed me in front of all of you?"

"He didn't slam you at all. Appeared to me as if he was teasing you. Playfully. Even challenging you to see if you could stand up to him. I think you two would make a good match. I feel something between…"

Shannon held up her hand before Kaitlyn could utter another word. "Do *not* tell me he's my destiny or I swear I will let out a scream that will bring this hotel down around us."

Kaitlyn held up her hands in mock surrender. "Ohhhkay. I won't say it. But if Mom was here…"

"Mom isn't here. And Max Devlin is not my destiny. For God's sake, I haven't even known him a day. You and Mom are too quick to jump on this destiny thing."

"Worked for Aidan and Lissa."

"That was different."

"How so?"

"I don't know, just different. They were different. Hell, Kait, we all felt their connection, and close your mouth right now because I know what you're going to say. There is no connection between me and Max Devlin. Nothing. Zip. I don't feel a damn thing. So quit comparing us to Aidan and Lissa. This whole conversation is ridiculous."

"And yet you're going out to dinner with him."

"He asked me to, said he didn't know anything about where to eat. Now you know Mom would have my hide if I left a newcomer to fend for himself."

"Uh huh." Kaitlyn crossed her arms, giving Shannon her classic *I'm right and you know it* look.

"You're a pain in the ass, you know that? Don't you have some event to plan?"

Nonplussed, Kaitlyn grinned. "Not really. Thought I'd just hang out here and see you and Max off to dinner."

Shannon rolled her eyes at her sister. They fought like this all the time. For as long as she could remember, she and Kaitlyn had tiffs. Sometimes shouting matches. Many times lots of weather was exchanged. Spring and fall storms…very volatile. Until their mother stepped in the middle and put an end to it.

But as quick as the storm rolled in, it blew itself out. She and Kaitlyn adored each other. Sparring was second nature to them. Shannon knew that Kaitlyn was just a little too in love with the idea of her brothers and sisters falling in love. She wished her sister would focus her attentions on finding a man for herself instead of playing matchmaker for everyone else.

"Oh look, here he comes," Kaitlyn announced, giggling like a schoolgirl.

Shannon rolled her eyes. As if Max were the King of England or something. He grinned as he approached. "How lucky can a guy get? Here are two of the most beautiful women in New Orleans."

Kaitlyn smiled. Shannon snorted and said, "Shall we go?"

"In a hurry?" he asked.

"Yes. My favorite television program is on tonight. Can't miss it."

"Ignore her, Max," Kaitlyn chimed in. "You two have a great time. Shannon knows all the best places to eat."

"Kaitlyn, would you like to come with us?" he asked.

Shannon glanced at her sister, sending her mental signals to say yes. The last thing she wanted was to be alone with Max tonight. She was already kicking herself for agreeing to have dinner with him without inviting one of the other family members along. Where was her brain?

"No, thank you. I already have plans. In fact, I'm late. Gotta run!" She waved and scurried to the elevators.

Traitor. Shannon knew Kaitlyn had no plans tonight. Matchmaking little sneak.

Resigned, she turned to Max. "What would you like to have tonight?"

He arched a brow and didn't say a word, but his lips curled in a smile that could only be described as sexually lethal.

"How about I just let you be in charge of…what I'm having tonight?" he suggested, the grin never leaving his face.

Ignoring the way he looked at her, she asked, "You're letting me decide? Wow, that's a first already. Sure you trust my judgment?"

"As it relates to food, yes."

"Fine. Let's go." She turned, wanting to hurry them along and hopefully keep her distance from Max, but he stayed in step beside her, resting his hand on her lower back as they moved to the doors. She nearly tripped over her shoes at the possessive feel of his hand on her, her skin on fire from his touch even though several layers of clothing separated his hand from her body.

Mentally cursing her traitorous body, she suffered him touching her as they headed outside and down the street. Solicitous to the point of great annoyance, he continued to touch her, directing her one way or the other with the slightest pressure of his hand against her back.

Really, it wasn't as if he knew where he was going. And she couldn't even move ahead of him because he kept pace with her no matter if she walked quickly or slowly. Damn, was this guy possessive or what?

Fortunately, the restaurant was only a couple blocks from the hotel. The day's heat still lingered and perspiration settled between her breasts, making her wish she'd changed into something cooler than her suit and blouse. As it was, the silk clung to her and she prayed desperately for the cool air conditioning of the restaurant. Otherwise, she might just have to strip.

And she'd just bet that Max would like that, too. Well, not a chance. She'd just perspire to death instead.

They walked inside the dimly lit restaurant. Why she chose Arnaud's was unfathomable. Most likely because it was close and she was hot. It had nothing to do with the ambience of romance that permeated every corner of the room. No, she sure as hell wouldn't have brought Max in here if she'd thought about it twice. The last thing she wanted to do was give him the wrong impression. Bad enough he had latched onto her hand earlier today and forced her rather windy reaction.

"Nice place," he said. And there went that hand again, gravitating to the small of her back as the maître d' approached.

"*Bon soir*, Francois," she said as the gray-mustached waiter hurried over.

"Mademoiselle Storm!" She'd known Francois her entire life. He had to be in his late sixties by now, and yet still filled with as much abundant energy as he'd been when she was a child. He was merely a little rounder and a lot grayer now than he was back then.

"We are so happy to see you here tonight!" He nodded and smiled at Max. "*Bon soir*, Monsieur. Would you care to be seated in the main restaurant, or a more private dining area?"

"Out here is fine, Francois." The last thing she wanted was to eat in a private dining room with Max. Definitely keep things public with him. Public, business-like and totally hands off.

They were seated at a corner table overlooking the street. She'd always loved sitting by the windows. The leaded glass caught and held the sun during the daylight hours, filtering the rays until a kaleidoscope of color cascaded through the windows and onto the floors. The atmosphere made her feel transported backward in time, when opulence and beauty was the norm of the day. She studied the mosaic floors, remembering coming here with her parents, counting each colorful tile while her parents had their own conversations.

When she looked up, Max was watching her. Neither smiling nor frowning, he looked as if he were studying her, measuring her, making some kind of decision about her.

Suddenly uncomfortable, she cleared her throat and signaled for their waiter. "Would you like a glass of wine?" she asked.

"How about a bottle?"

Shannon had been drinking wine since she was old enough to hold a glass. It was a matter of culture here. And she was damn near expert in the different types of wine, including what had a fancy label and expensive price tag, but no flavor, and how to spot a wine amateur in a matter of seconds. She sat back and offered a smug smile. "Sure. You go ahead and order."

He arched a brow and took the wine list from the waiter, scanned it quickly, and ordered a bottle of her favorite Chardonnay.

Well, hell. No amateur there. Or maybe it was just a lucky guess.

"I take it you don't object to my choice?" he asked, smirking.

Why did she have this sudden urge to slap that smile off his face? "No. It's fine."

They sipped their drinks and ordered dinner. Shannon stared out the window, but Max looked only at her. Damned disconcerting, too. Did she have a zit on her nose or something? She'd never met someone so incredibly intense, or so blatantly interested in just looking at her.

Despite the air conditioning in the restaurant, her body heated, all too aware of his wandering looks

"So, what kind of PR campaign ideas do you have?" she asked, hoping if she could get him talking about business, he'd quit looking at her as if *she* was his intended meal.

"I don't want to talk business tonight. We can do that tomorrow."

"What do you want to talk about, then?" And if he hadn't wanted to discuss public relations for the hotel, why the hell had he invited her to dinner? Maybe she didn't really want to know the answer to that question, after all.

"I want to talk about you."

"I don't."

His green eyes turned more golden. "You don't strike me as the shy type."

"I'm not. But my personal life isn't any of your business."

"Oh, but you're wrong. It's every bit my business," he answered, then took a long swallow of the wine. She watched, his Adam's apple undulating with the movement of his throat. When he finished, he licked his lips. She tried not to be enticed by the flicking tip of his tongue around that sensual mouth of his. "I have to know about you, about your family, their history and how it all relates to The Rising Storm."

"My family's personal life has nothing to do with The Rising Storm."

"A good public relations campaign," he started, accentuating the *good* part as if what she'd done so far had been crap, "starts from the ground and moves up. That means your family's background and how they became hoteliers is the basis with which we start our plan."

Did she look like an idiot? "No, the PR is strictly for the hotel/casino venture. The people of Louisiana have heard about the Storm family before. We've run that public relations gamut many times."

He poured more wine for them. "That's fine for Louisiana. Do you only want the people of Louisiana visiting your hotel, or do you want this campaign to reach out nationally, even internationally?"

She gripped the stem of her glass and tried not to grit her teeth. "We're way too small an organization to branch out internationally."

His grin made her heart race. What would that smile look like if it had been turned on her in wicked passion? An involuntary shudder passed through her. Why the hell was she thinking these kind of thoughts about him? Really, this was all too much. She mentally summoned a cooling breeze, hopefully subtle enough that Max would assume it was simply the restaurant's air conditioning.

"You'll never be successful if you don't think big, Shannon. International travelers are always looking for unique vacation spots. New Orleans has a charm and old-world ambience that is unique to Louisiana. Coupled with the magic present here, you've got a huge potential market you haven't begun to tap into yet."

Magic? She almost laughed. He really had no idea what kind of magic whirled around him. It irked her that she had never thought beyond a statewide campaign. Max was a big dreamer, obviously. Head in the clouds. She was more grounded in reality.

"Yes, of course I've thought of taking public relations through a national sweep. But if you'd bother to read my outline—"

"I've read it. Your plan is only to launch statewide at first."

"Yes, I know what it says. I wrote it, remember?" She knew she sounded like a shrew, but frankly didn't care. She'd warned Logan that bringing an outsider in would only screw things up. "The long-range planning includes a nationwide program, but not until we gauge the success of the statewide campaign."

"Too slow. Need to step it up and launch nationwide immediately."

"I don't agree. It's best to begin conservatively, then see how the numbers pan out after the first six months."

He picked up a breadstick and took a bite, then pointed it at her. "Bullshit. If you wait, you waste momentum. You'll get the biggest hits in a grand opening launch. Take your pre-opening and grand opening and do it nationwide. Do some charity events, get the Storm name out there as philanthropists. Get your parents or Logan to sit on a board of some national and international corporations. Then set a quick timeline and take it worldwide. We could even do an international launch that coincides with the nationwide. In fact, because of the time involved in all the language translations, we should start on that right away."

She tapped her foot on the tile floor, grateful for the wine to calm her down. As it was, her blood was boiling, frustration giving her an overwhelming desire to whack Max upside the head with the empty wine bottle. He clearly wasn't listening. She was in charge here!

Their dinner arrived, but Shannon could only pick at the delectable trout meunière, her appetite shattered with questions, insecurities and general irritation at having to deal with Max Devlin. He, however, had no such issues, and wolfed down his bloody rare filet mignon like a man starving. He didn't even seem uncomfortable with her cold silence.

Were all men so completely clueless as to a woman's emotional state, or was it just Max's head that was so thick?

"Aren't you hungry?" he asked, apparently noticing for the first time that she hadn't eaten.

"Not really."

He waved his fork toward her. "You're too skinny. You need some meat to fatten you up a bit."

She snorted. That was the first time she'd heard any man complain. And what was wrong with her body, anyway? She wasn't the least bit thin, in fact thought herself average in build. Not heavy, not thin, just average for her height. She played tennis, she ran, and stayed in shape. Mainly to keep her energy level high, but she admittedly loved to run. Fast, hard and at great distances. Running gave her time to unwind, to think, to release the stress she always carried inside her.

"My body is fine."

He leaned back in the chair and slung one arm casually over the arm. "Yes, it's more than fine. At least what I can see of it."

"Your comments are inappropriate."

"You liked it, though, didn't you?"

What an egotistical asshole! How dare he assume that because he complimented her body that she'd find him the least bit appealing! "I think this conversation is over, Mr. Devlin." Enough was enough and she had her limits.. Maybe her body liked what he said, but the professional inside her didn't. She waved the waiter over and asked for the check.

"I'll take care of that," he said, opening his wallet and pulling out his credit card.

"No, it'll go on The Rising Storm's expense account. This was a business dinner, where we had a business discussion." And that's all she'd remember about tonight.

He shrugged and put his card away. "Suit yourself, but I'd like to take you out on my own dime sometime."

Not if he were the last man on earth and she was desperate to the point of begging. "I don't think that's a good idea. Let's just keep things between us strictly business." Which meant quit looking at her like he was still hungry.

"Oh, I think we've already progressed way beyond strictly business."

Who the hell had he had dinner with tonight? They hadn't touched on personal issues at all, other than the fact he'd personally insulted her business acumen.

She signed the check and stood, waving to Francois and heading out the door. Max, of course, was right behind her. As soon as the front door shut she turned to him, whispering so the few people walking around couldn't hear. "Look, Max. I don't know what you think is going on between us, but let's get it straight right now. We have a business relationship, and that's all we'll ever have. I don't mix business with pleasure. Ever."

His gaze lingered on her mouth when she spoke. Dammit, why did her nipples have to harden? She really needed to get laid soon, because for some reason her idiotic hormones had suddenly decided to target Max Devlin as if he really *was* the last man on earth.

"Don't you feel what's between us, Shannon?" he said, reaching for her arm and trailing his hand up and down her wrist. When he slipped his fingers inside the cuff of her jacket and rested them on her racing pulse, she wished she had argued harder with Logan about inviting Max here.

She shook off the feelings of confusion. "I don't feel a damn thing for you but irritation, Max. Let go of me."

"I don't think you really want me to let go of you."

"I don't think you really know what can happen to you if you mess with me."

He arched a brow but held on to her wrist, rubbing the skin back and forth until she broke out in a sweat.

"You want me to mess with you. In every way imaginable."

Really, the man was insufferable. What an incredible ego to think that all he had to do was flash his sexy grin at her and she'd spread her legs. Her body might respond to him, but her mind fought him every step of the way. "I don't want a damn thing from you, Max. In fact, I can end your contract with The Rising Storm in a heartbeat. One conversation with Logan and Aidan and not only will you be out of a job, you're very likely to get your ass kicked."

His lips wavered as if he were fighting a smile. "I don't think you'll do that."

She wanted to scream. Instead, she lowered her voice and spoke slowly, hoping it would penetrate his thick, Neanderthal skull. "Try me. Now, let go."

He continued to hold her arm. The strangest thing was, he wasn't holding onto her tight enough that she couldn't break free. He *wanted* her to pull away. But damned if she'd do what he expected. He'd thrown down the gauntlet, dammit, and she was going to stand firm until *he* backed off.

He inhaled deeply, then met her gaze. She rocked back on her heels at the intensity of his eyes. More golden than green now, narrowed slits that were filled with a palpable passion that shot between her legs. She moistened, desire seeping from her slit and wetting her panties. Her pussy throbbed deep inside, her breasts swelled, and her lips parted as she struggled to find her next breath.

"You don't wear perfume," he whispered, lazily running his thumb over her palm, then entwining his fingers with hers. "I can smell your sweet scent. You're aroused."

He could do no such thing! It wasn't possible. She didn't want these thoughts in her head, didn't want her body to react the way it was. "No!" she cried. Giving up on her earlier mental challenge, she pulled her arm away and turned from him, desperate to return to the hotel so she could slide into the safety of her car and go home.

Home, where he wouldn't follow, where she could get her head on straight, and get her body in line with the here and now. What the hell was happening to her?

Not bothering to turn to see if he was following, she hurried toward the hotel. As soon as she crossed the main entrance, she signaled for the valet to bring her car. She released the breath that she'd been holding, then finally turned around.

Max was nowhere to be found. He hadn't followed her, nor was he still standing on the corner where they'd spoken.

Where was he? She looked around, but couldn't see him. It was late, and the French Quarter was never empty. Still, he stood out enough that she should be able to easily spot him among the tourists.

She had no idea where he'd gone. Frankly, she didn't care. The only thing she felt was relief that she'd managed to extricate herself from whatever weird spell he'd cast on her.

The valet brought her car and she slipped inside, locked the doors, and sped away, opening the sunroof for some air. She hoped the drive to the condo she shared with Kaitlyn would help clear her head. Her sister would know immediately that something had happened, unless she emptied her mind and her emotions of everything having to do with Max Devlin.

She drove out of the city and into the secluded part of town where she and Kaitlyn lived. She loved the cooler feel to the heavily wooded area, and even though she lived in a complex with hundreds of other people, she still enjoyed the dense trees and secluded forest.

Pulling quickly into her parking spot, she stepped out, then froze as she heard a rustling in the trees behind her. With a quick turn, she scanned the area. The parking lot was well lit, but the forested area beyond was pitch black.

Instinctively her thumb searched for and found the panic button attached to her car alarm. Ready to punch it if she saw someone coming from the trees, her heart leapt into her throat at the sight of a quick moving animal darting briefly out of the woods.

It stopped right outside the tree line. Shannon's heart pounded against her ribs. What the hell was it? Some kind of dog?

No dog had yellow eyes. Eyes that glowed, and seemed to be staring straight at her. It had a long snout and gray and white fur, but that was no dog. She couldn't move, afraid the slightest movement would cause the animal to strike. A low growl emanated from the creature, and it took one step forward toward her.

She hit the panic button and the shrill car alarm sounded. In her hazy panic, she barely even registered the earsplitting sound.

At least it scared off the animal, who turned and bounded into the woods, disappearing just as quickly as it had appeared.

She punched the button and silenced the alarm, her pulse speeding so hard it made her dizzy. Flopping back into the front seat of the car, she fought for control over her breathing, trying to settle her nerves.

When her legs felt steady enough to stand, she got out of the car, set the alarm, and walked briskly to the front door of her condo.

During the short trip to the front door, she felt as if the wolf still lurked within the trees, watching her. She could actually feel its eyes on her, but refused to turn around and look.

As if she hadn't had enough turmoil today, now she had to face the fact that she'd nearly been attacked by a wolf.

A wolf. She'd never heard of wolves prowling the woods here. Hell, she didn't even know there were wolves in New Orleans.

What a fitting way to end an already miserable day.

Chapter Three

✍

Max watched Shannon make a frantic dash to her front door. Hidden safely among the dense trees, he knew he wouldn't be seen by anyone who happened to investigate the shrill sound of her car alarm.

Figured, no one even came out. Not that she'd been in any danger. He'd never hurt her. But it had been stupid to walk out of the forest like that. What had he hoped to accomplish? That she'd instinctively know who he was? That she'd come to him, embrace him in his wolf form and tell him that she wanted to be with him? Or even better, he could have partially shifted, leaving himself half human so that she could have recognized him. That would surely have endeared her to him immediately.

Hey, babe, lookin' for a hairy guy who likes quiet walks on the beach and the occasional piece of raw meat? Are you up for a little howling at the moon? And how do you feel about sex with a half man, half wolf? Pretty hot, huh?

Damn, if that was the best plan he had, he was screwed, and not in a good way. The problem was she blew away his normally clear, logical approach to things. All he wanted to do when he saw her was rip her clothes off piece by piece, preferably with his teeth, and lick every square inch of her body.

Twice.

He kept his eyes on her as she slipped inside and closed the door. Probably tossed some furniture in front of it too, just for extra safety. He'd seen the look on her face when she'd spotted him. That wide-eyed fear in her eyes. She knew nothing about his kind.

This was going to take some time. Gain her trust first, then revelations. Not the other way around. He was moving too fast and he knew it.

Try telling his body to be patient. It wasn't listening to his head. At least not the head located on the upper part of his body.

No sense lingering here. It hadn't been difficult to follow her home since she drove along the tree-lined streets. Not too far from the hotel either.

After she'd run off at the restaurant, he figured he'd better give her some space. So he'd headed for the nearest wooded area and shifted, needing a run to clear his own head. And while he was at it, thought he might as well as try to pick up the scent of other packs.

Problem was, the only scent he focused on was Shannon's. He'd picked up her unique scent when she drove past him, and he'd followed, ending up in front of her condo, no doubt scaring the hell out of her.

Enough. Pushing thoughts of Shannon from his mind, he took off in a run. The moonless night left him free to roam at will without the chance of anyone from the nearby roads spotting him. He ran for miles, stretching the travel kinks from his legs and breathing in the scented night air.

He'd stop occasionally, sniff the area around him to see if he could pick up a pack's scent. Nothing yet. But then again he didn't expect to find many, if any, wolves in this area.

The thought both excited him and punched him with a loneliness he hadn't expected. He was alone here, and if he found a pack and challenged the alpha for leadership, then he'd have a new family. But his current family resided in Boston, and he had to adjust to the fact he was on his own now.

His brother Jason had to do it when he moved from the pack to follow his political career in Washington. And he'd adjusted just fine. Max would, too. Besides, they'd known this was coming from the time they were young pups. The Devlin family was well connected in politics and industry, and it was their prime goal to branch out in all geographic areas and establish dominance. This project in New Orleans with the Storm family was just what they'd been looking for as a means to gain a stronghold in the south.

After wandering a bit, Max came upon a lake. While there were some heavily populated areas around the calm water, there were also plenty of places with dense trees and unoccupied land. He noted his surroundings and marked his scent. First off, to find it again, second, to alert any other packs in the area that there was a new wolf in town.

He spotted a few houses along the way, nestled deep within the trees and no neighbors within visual distance. Skirting around the front, he noted the For Sale sign on one.

There was a dense wooded area right behind the house. He traveled within, feeling at home with the smells and sounds of the forest. He picked up a scent of wolves, too. Faint, but there nevertheless. Whether they were still here or not he didn't know, but at least they had been here once before.

Yes, this place would be perfect. A huge two-story house, with a porch that surrounded the entire perimeter. Perfect. He'd come back, maybe even bring Shannon with him to see how she reacted. After all, wherever he set up house, she'd be living with him, so it was important she liked the place too.

He returned where he had changed and hidden his clothes, shifting back to his human form. He'd made sure to shift into wolf form far beyond the busy French Quarter, leaving his clothes near a crop of trees that hid him from view. After a quick walk back to the hotel, he stepped inside and hurried to his room, ready for a shower and some sleep. He'd already prowled half the night away, and tomorrow he'd have to do battle with Shannon over their public relations program again.

He couldn't wait.

Her aroma still clung to him, a musky flavor unique to her alone. She wore no perfume. He liked that, preferring to smell her natural fragrance. The rest of that expensive crap they sold in stores just hid a woman's emotional state from him. With Shannon, he knew exactly what she was feeling. It showed in her eyes, her facial expressions, body movements and the primal scent she gave off that hardened him just thinking about it.

Changing his mind about showering, he flopped naked on the bed and turned out the lights, preferring traces of Shannon to linger on him. He'd shower in the morning.

The drapes were open, the stars and the glow from the street lights visible in the night sky. He propped the pillows up and looked outside, wishing he were still in wolf form and running alongside the lake.

Restlessness still flowed through him. That and the smell of Shannon would keep him awake the remainder of the night, unless he got some relief. His cock rose, his balls heavy and tight. He was near desperate to mate, but the woman he wanted, the only woman he wanted, had run from him like the hounds of hell were chasing her.

Sometimes he hated the way wolves mated. Once settling on a mate, she was it. No doubt about it, and no one else would satisfy him. He'd chosen Shannon…no, that wasn't quite right. A mate was destined, a primal urge to be with one certain person. Shannon was that person and what was fated couldn't be changed. Until she was ready, he'd have to do without.

That would change soon enough, but not tonight. He fisted his rigid length and slid his hand over his shaft, wishing it were her cool, soft hands on his cock. He closed his eyes, imagining how it would be between them. She'd undress for him while he stood hard and waiting for her. He could tell from her scent that she was aroused, her slit swelling, opening to receive him, her clit revealing itself, standing ready for his tongue.

Squeezing his shaft hard, he groaned as drops of pre-come slid over his fingers. Circling the head with his thumb, he spread the silken fluid over his cockhead, imagining the hot moisture was Shannon's warm tongue sliding over the ridged tip, teasing him by flicking it around the sensitive head before enveloping him between her lips and sucking him, taking him deeper and deeper, over and over again until he couldn't hold back and shot a torrent of come down her throat.

Would she be docile in bed, a meek kitten who waited for a man to tell her what to do? Or would she be a voracious lover, demanding that he satisfy her, commanding him to plunge deeply inside until she screamed in ecstasy?

He knew the answer. The latter. She was an alpha female, that's why he selected her, that's why they were to be mated. Only a strong female could lead a pack with him, could run alongside him and raise strong cubs.

The movements of his hand increased, his mind awash in visuals of her naked body underneath him, her nipples glowing in the moonlight, standing up like hard, mountainous peaks and begging for his tongue to lick at them. Her turquoise eyes sparkled like hard diamonds, without words telling him what she wanted, what she needed.

His hand moved faster over his shaft, stroking from base to tip. His balls grew tighter, hugging his body, throbbing, aching for release. Damn, he wanted his cock inside Shannon's pussy, not in his hand. He wanted her on her knees, her bare ass spread before him, the lips of her cunt wet and ready for him to drive hard inside her. He needed to be inside her, and he would be. Everywhere. He'd take control of her and take her in every way possible.

This wasn't the way he wanted to do it, but he had no choice. Images of her doing the same thing took front and center in his mind. Suddenly, she was driving her fingers into her wet pussy and fucking herself as he watched. Her free hand roamed over her breasts, tugging at her nipples until

Jaci Burton

they stood like sharp points. She thrust her hips against him, a silent invitation to take what he saw.

With a loud groan, he came in hard, quick spurts, visions of shooting deep inside Shannon intensifying his orgasm. Spent, he lay there panting, wishing she were there with him. He'd take her into his arms and hold her close, possessively, knowing then and there that she belonged to him.

He stared outside, formulating his plan for the next several weeks.

Sure as hell this scenario wasn't going to work for long. The last thing he wanted was to sniff around Shannon during the day and come back here at night to release the sexual buildup. No, that was not how this was going to play out.

He closed his eyes, hoping he could get a couple hours sleep before dawn. If he could keep his mind off Shannon long enough to drift off.

And yet, visions of her invaded his mind. In her bed, cream silk sheets caressing her body, her sable hair fanned out on her pillow. He felt her, almost as if he stood in her bedroom.

He'd never sleep tonight.

* * * * *

Shannon shifted, burrowing further under the covers. A thick fog covered her bedroom, revealing only the wrought iron bed upon which she lay.

A dream. Clearly she was asleep and having one of those *I'm dreaming and I know it but it feels real so I'm gonna enjoy it anyway* kind of dreams.

Funny how in one's dreams all senses heightened. The cool sheets rubbed against her naked breasts, her nipples tingling in response. When she shifted, satin rubbed against her sex. Her pussy tightened, heated, that familiar and sweet sense of arousal making her wish she wasn't lying alone in the middle of her bed.

48

The fog began to lift. Okay, so she wasn't alone in her bed.

The wolf, the one she'd seen outside the condo, lay at her feet.

"Go away," she hissed, as if the very act of saying *shoo* would have an impact on a wolf.

Besides, this was a dream, and in her dreams she was in control, just the way she liked her real life. It couldn't hurt her in her dream.

The wolf didn't budge. Instead, a low growl emanated from its throat as if responding to her request to leave with *I'll leave when I'm damn good and ready and not a minute before.*

So now what? Were they going to have a staring contest? What the hell was the damn wolf doing in her dream anyway? Why couldn't she be having fantasies of some rich, handsome movie star sneaking into her bedroom at dawn and fucking the daylights out of her?

The wolf stretched, then stood, creeping slowly between her outstretched legs. Its eyes glowed an eerie green and yellow. Okay, that was unusual, and yet hauntingly familiar. Who had eyes that color?

Oh, God. She knew.

In the instant her mind made the connection, the wolf changed, becoming not quite human, yet no longer fully a wolf. And in that change she saw clear human characteristics that could only be attributed to one man. His face was more that of a wolf's than a man's, his elongated snout and long tongue licking at his very prominent teeth. But his body was a man's, partially covered in fur, fingers more like claws, but definitely a man's body.

A man's naked body.

Max.

Well, as weird dreams went, this one had to top them all. After all, it had been one hell of an odd day. No wonder her mind was filled with Max and the wolf. And in her warped brain cells, obviously the two had merged into one, creating this freaky apparition at the foot of her bed.

Not a turnoff, either. In fact, the intense way he looked at her, the sight of him half covered in fur and half naked…okay, it turned her on.

Big time.

"You want me," he whispered, his husky voice like secrets in the dark. Funny, he talked normally, just like Max, despite the fact his face was partially wolfen.

"Yes." Hell, why not? It was just a dream. If she couldn't have some no-holds-barred fun in her dreams, where could she?

"You like being in control, like dominating every situation."

Now he was talking. "Yes, I do."

"That ends with me, Shannon. I'm in control here, I will be your master in the bedroom. And what's more…you'll like it that way."

No fucking way in reality, but here…sure. She didn't answer, figuring he wasn't expecting her to. Besides, she couldn't very well speak since her heart now lodged somewhere in her throat, pounding, swelling, cutting off her breath as he ripped the covers away, exposing her naked flesh to his gaze.

He licked his lips. His tongue was amazingly long. Her mind sailed in all kinds of naughty directions. Instinctively, her hips rose off the bed. When his head shot up and his feral gaze met hers, he smiled.

"I know what you want."

Of course, he knew what she wanted. It was her dream after all.

"You want me to lick you. I've dreamed of tasting you, since before we even met."

Before? Okay, she wasn't going to ask him to explain that one. Dreams made no sense anyway. "Then lick my pussy."

His thick brows arched. "Oh, I will. In my own good time. Remember, I'm in control here. Not you."

With his gaze firmly planted on her sex, he grasped her legs and pulled them apart. She realized he looked directly between them, his tongue snaking out and licking over his lips. The drawing pull of desire warmed her lower belly, centering her, preparing her. A sense of urgency enveloped her, making her want, need, that release that he promised.

He sat back on his heels, his face more and more recognizable as Max and less like the wolf's. But he still retained the partial wolfen features, especially that glorious tongue. Already, she could feel it on her, covering her sex, lapping up her juices. And he hadn't even touched her yet.

His hands changed shape too, becoming more human in appearance, the claws sheathing until his nails took on regular shape. He reached for her feet, pulling one onto his lap, nestling the flat of her foot against his hard cock.

And what a cock it was. Her eyes grew wider as she focused on his shaft for the first time. *Mon dieu, c'est magnifique!*

A sound came from his throat. Some kind of contented growl? His sensual onslaught against her body was nearly more than she could handle. His scent, his voice, especially coupled with the slow, deliberately sexy way he massaged her feet. Then he did the unexpected, lifting her foot and licking her toes with his incredible tongue.

She nearly shot to the ceiling at the feel of his warm, wet tongue sliding over her toes and foot. Good lord, that was an amazing sensation!

He didn't stop there, either. With agonizing precision, he licked his way up and over her ankles, calves, concentrating on the back of her legs until she shivered uncontrollably. Damn, the back of her knees were an erogenous zone. Had she known that before?

Of course not. No man had ever taken the time to lick the backs of her knees. How could she have known that?

Max did. Thoroughly exploring every inch of her body, he was on an expedition of discovery, and tasting every inch of her skin was a quest toward the ultimate finish line.

"Hurry," she urged, desperate for his tongue to touch that burning spot between her legs.

"Mmm hmm," was his only response.

Finally, he reached her aching pussy, his mouth and that fantastic tongue mere inches away. But instead of diving in like she expected, he moved up and over her sex, planting kisses on both her hip bones and sliding his tongue into her belly button.

"Dammit, not *there*!" Really, did he need a roadmap?

He looked up at her and grinned. "I know exactly where I'm going. It's not the destination, Shannon, it's the journey."

"Bullshit. Lick my pussy."

He only laughed and ignored her. Well, hell. This was her dream. How come she wasn't getting it the way she wanted it?

"You are used to being in control. You'll get exactly what you want, love, but not yet."

If she was awake, she'd kick him. But right now he held the magic key and she'd just keep her mouth shut and her feet to herself. At least until she came. Then she'd let him have it, and not in a good way.

He reached for her breasts, and it was like a near-death experience when his fingers swept over her throbbing nipples. She arched her back, giving him access to the twin globes. And he took advantage, maneuvering his way over her body so that his mouth rested in her cleavage.

Without her having to ask him this time, his tongue snaked out and licked first one, then the other crest.

She whimpered. She never whimpered. But, oh, was his tongue heaven. Long and warm, he licked her, then covered one bud with his mouth, drawing the nub between his teeth and gently nibbling at her, sucking her nipple inside his mouth until it pressed between his tongue and the roof of his mouth.

A tight coiling began deep inside her pussy. Knowing this was a dream allowed her to free the magic ready to burst inside her. The wind blew through the room, papers flying everywhere. The fog that had settled around the bed like a wall dissipated, leaving in its wake a drenching downpour that did nothing to cool her heated flesh.

Quickly, he moved down her body as if he sensed her need. Finally.

She closed her eyes and let out a cry of delight when his tongue lapped over her swollen slit. His growls of pleasure only heightened the sensations spiraling through her. She reached for him, twining her fingers into his hair, not wanting him to move from that delicious spot he covered with his long, hot tongue.

He swept over her flesh, alternatively licking and lightly nibbling, then covered her throbbing clit with his mouth and sucked. That was all it took. The buildup to the crescendo that had threatened to crash down over her came now in full force with the gentle suction of his lips over her clit.

"Yes! Yes! Oh, God, yes, like that! Oh, *mon dieu*, Max, I'm coming!"

She grasped the wrought-iron headboard behind her and shrieked. Her orgasm came in a torrent that sent the wind lashing through the room, the rain flowing sideways as she cried out her climax, her fluids drenching him more than the sudden storm. Her hips continued to rise and fall with the sensations coursing through her, and she fought for breath as she rode out the pleasure.

But before she had a chance to still the rapid beating of her heart, he flipped her over onto all fours, licking his way down her back.

And lower.

He moistened her anus with his fabulous tongue, and sparks of renewed desire shot through her. Oh, God, what was he doing to her? No one had ever touched her there, and definitely hadn't licked her there. The sensation was overpowering, so incredibly erotic she almost came again.

He moved against her, his cock slipping between her buttocks and rubbing the sensitive rosette.

She knew then what she wanted.

God help her, she wanted it, too. This *was* just a dream, right?

With a light nip of his teeth against her shoulder, he eased himself between the tight muscles of her anus, slipping gently inside her.

His cock was huge, filling her, expanding within her heated passage.

Pleasure like she'd never experienced before arced through her. Max clenched her hips and drove harder, embedding his cock fully inside her small channel.

She cried out at the exquisitely painful pleasure, moving her ass against him to tell him she wanted more.

He gave her more. Harder, deeper, until she was whimpering and completely out of control.

Reaching between her legs, she caressed her engorged clit, rubbing in frantic circles in time to his repeated thrusts.

"You wanted this, didn't you?" he asked, his voice hard, gritty and turning her on more than she thought possible. "You wanted to be a little naughty. You need a man who will tap into your darkest desires, Shannon. Tell me this is what you want."

"Yes," she cried, hating to admit he was right, but knowing he gave her exactly what she needed. "Harder!"

He complied eagerly, and she wished she could watch his face, wondering if he felt the same way she did.

Completely overwhelmed, and nearing the edge of reason.

"Fuck my ass, Max," she groaned, slipping two of her fingers into her drenched pussy, feeling the muscles of her vagina surround them. She felt his cock moving in and out of her ass, and fucked herself harder, faster, until blinding light and unbearable sensations caused her to shut her eyes tight.

She came in a torrent, screaming out his name and driving her fingers deeper into her spasming cunt. Max tensed, then howled as his seed filled her.

But it didn't end. She kept coming, bucking back to meet his renewed thrusts until her limbs would no longer support her.

Max kissed her back, her neck, licking and biting her lightly. She dropped to the bed, unable to move. A languid laziness came over her, and she relaxed completely.

Then a shrill scream resounded.

Shannon blinked her eyes open. The room was completely dry. The alarm clock buzzed in loud staccato bursts. Realizing she still had a death grip on the iron headboard, she released her hold, leaned over and shut off the alarm.

Dawn filtered through the partially opened drapes of her window.

The covers had been pushed to the end of the bed, and she was drenched in sweat. Her pussy still throbbed with the pleasurable aftereffects of her orgasms. At least that part had been real.

"Holy shit," she whispered, taking a quick glance around the room as if she fully expected to see Max, or a wolf, or some combination of both, crouched in a corner.

He wasn't there. Of course he wasn't there, because she had been dreaming.

A dream that had culminated in two blindsiding orgasms that still had her legs trembling and her pulse racing.

"Wow." She couldn't help the words of wonder that spilled from her lips. Never had a dream felt so real. Never had her orgasms felt so amazing. If that had been a dream, she wanted one like that every night. She rested her elbows on her knees and dropped her chin into her hands, pondering whether she'd actually be able to get out of bed.

No choice there. She had to get up and go to work.

After she showered and dressed, she went in search of coffee, desperate for the clarity the caffeine could provide. Entering the kitchen, she found Kaitlyn already dressed. Her sister poured a steaming cup and handed it to her, then grinned.

"I'd ask if it was good for you, but from what I heard it was."

If it was anyone but Kaitlyn, she'd blush from the roots of her hair to the tips of her toes. But she shared everything with her sister. "I had what could only be described as a seriously hot wet dream."

"Obviously. Because I've never known the sound of the alarm clock to make you howl with pleasure," Kaitlyn said with a wink. "Care to share?"

"It was weird," she said, savoring the crisp flavor of the strong brew.

"All dreams are weird. This one must have been one helluva humdinger."

"I'll say. Remember that wolf I told you I saw last night?"

"Uh huh."

"It was in my bedroom, on my bed."

Kaitlyn arched a raven brow. "You had sex with a wolf in your dream?"

"No, silly. Well, sort of. Not really, though."

"Oh, this should be good," Kaitlyn said, pulling a stool up to the breakfast bar and perching half-on, half-off. "Okay, I'm listening."

Shannon shrugged, realizing if she mentioned Max as part of her dream, there'd be no end to the matchmaking. "The wolf took on the form of a man. Kind of half man, half creature."

Kaitlyn leaned forward, clearly interested in the word man. "Anyone we know?"

"No."

"Was he hot?"

"Hell yes, he was hot. Hot and half wolf. Powerful, damn talented too, if you know what I mean."

"I know exactly what you mean. See? I've always told you that you watch too many horror films. Too much sex and violence."

Shannon laughed. "It wasn't like that. The wolf was really just a sexy man. With a very long tongue."

Kaitlyn's eyes widened. "Wish I had dreams like that."

Shannon wished she had them more often. Every night would be good. She felt more at ease this morning than she had in months. Nothing like a good orgasm to start the day right.

Now if only she could manage to look Max Devlin in the eye when she saw him this morning, without thinking of him as part wolf.

But ooh la la, that tongue! She doubted that visual would ever leave her mind.

Which meant facing Max was going to take some fortitude on her part. For more reasons than one.

Chapter Four

৯১

Something about Max Devlin bothered the hell out of Shannon.

Okay, maybe more than one thing.

Not only was he arrogant, evidenced by the fact they'd been arguing for two days about the public relations plan. But there were other annoyances, too.

Like how he stood too close to her, invading her personal space, making her feel...

Feel what? Uncomfortable? Kind of, but not really in a *get the hell away from me* kind of way. More in a *damn you for making me notice you* kind of way. And the way her body more than responded to being near him didn't help at all. What was wrong with her anyway?

The absolute last thing she wanted or needed was an attraction to another corporate go-getter, someone climbing his way to the top. The last man she'd been involved with had used her as a rung on his ladder to success. Good thing her heart hadn't been involved at the time, and maybe that should have been a clear indicator that something was amiss. But she hadn't recognized the signs, hadn't noticed how he was more interested in her family and their position in the business world than he was in her.

Well, after that disaster it wasn't going to happen again. Men were good for one-time fucking, occasional social dates, only when absolutely necessary, and that was it.

She didn't want to have dreams about them, didn't want her body to respond to them, and sure as hell didn't want to be thinking nonstop about them.

No, not *them*. Him. Max. He was the only one occupying her mind the past couple days.

Like right now, as he leaned back in a chair in the small conference room, her public relations program in one hand, a red pen in the other. Slash mark after slash mark bled all over the pages. So deep in concentration, he didn't even notice her pacing a hole in the rug behind him, stopping every few minutes to heave a disgusted sigh as she looked over his shoulder and watched him massacring her work.

"Couple more hours and I think we'll have the national and international program ready to go."

"Uh huh." She stood directly behind him, wondering if her small hands would fit around his thick neck. Probably not. Too bad.

"You'll like these ideas. Trust me."

"Uh huh." She didn't even want to read them, in fact after days of work, her first intent would be to toss his ideas right in the circular file near her desk. This was her campaign, dammit, and they were going to run it her way, no matter what Max Devlin thought.

She wondered if there was a good voodoo-curse store around the corner? Nothing life-threatening, of course. Some genital warts would be nice sprouting up on Max's dick.

He whirled around in the chair and she took a quick step back. Pinning her with his gaze, he smiled and said, "And I owe you an apology."

"Huh?"

"An apology." Waving the binder in front of her, he said, "I underestimated your talent. Your statewide public relations blitz is really good. You have a keen eye for what will capture the public's attention."

Okay, maybe just crabs, then...not warts. "Thank you."

So she'd take a look at his notes, and then she'd throw them in the trash. She took the binder and sat across the oval table from him, pouring through his comments. Occasionally she'd look up to find him staring at her, but she ignored him, concentrating instead on what was obviously sheer brilliance.

Okay, so he knew public relations. More than knew it. Especially nationwide programs, not to mention international. In a few hours of scribbles he'd outlined what would, essentially, catapult The Rising Storm into one of the top hotel/casino chains in the nation.

No wonder Lissa thought so highly of him, and why Logan had agreed to bring him down here to work with her.

She had to admit defeat on this one. He knew way more than she did, at least about running their PR program outside the state. "This is fantastic."

He grinned, and her heart slammed against her ribs. "You think so? Great. Do you think it's doable in the time parameters I outlined?"

"Maybe. Might need a little tweaking, but definitely close to the deadline dates."

"Good. And now that I look at your statewide plan, I think you're right. We can start the blitz statewide, then in the next quarter take it nationally."

He agreed with her? Damn, she should have played the lottery today. So maybe he wasn't the big bad wolf. She stood, figuring she'd better get back to her office. Max rose and skirted the table, stopping in front of her.

Lord, he smelled good. Like fresh sunshine and the crisp, warm outdoors in the summer. She didn't want to stare at the pulse throbbing in his neck, or wonder if his skin would taste salty if she licked there.

He cleared his throat and she tilted her head back, meeting his gaze. The yellow flecks seemed to dance through his eyes, like spots of sun filtering a green meadow.

Whenever she stood close to him, her magic churned within her, like it wanted to erupt all around them. She fought hard to keep it contained.

"Your eyes change colors sometimes," he said, tucking one of her errant hairs behind her ear. "The blue clouds over, grows darker, like a squall is brewing."

Oh, it was brewing all right. She shuddered at the brush of his fingers against her ear, wondering what he'd do if she let loose her powers and showed him what she was capable of. Probably run screaming from the room. Wouldn't that be an interesting sight? Max Devlin running for his life.

Then again, he didn't strike her as the type of man who'd run from anything.

And she liked him better when they were arguing. Then she could easily keep her distance. This...this she didn't like. His easy smile, the way his hair curled against the back of his neck, making her want to reach out and caress the dark locks, the way his gaze focused on hers in a way that had nothing to do with business.

When he was nice to her she wanted to give in and...

And do what? Grab him, kiss him, throw him down on top of the conference room table and have her way with him?

Oh, no. She was *not* going there! Better to keep her lusty thoughts about Max confined to her dreams. Much safer that way.

"Shannon, there's something I want to talk to you about. I—"

"There you are!" Kaitlyn threw the doors open and hurried toward them. "You two going to stay holed up in here all night? There's a party to prepare for, you know."

Shannon quickly stepped back, thankful for the interruption. Yet a part of her wanted to hear what Max had been about to say. Probably better that she didn't know. She threw a smile at her sister. "Yes, we're aware there's a party tonight."

"It's the big PR launch for the hotel, you know." Kaitlyn rolled her eyes as if everyone should be as excited about an event as she always was.

"And it's going to be fantastic," Max said. "I'm looking forward to it."

Kaitlyn glowed. "Thanks. Me too. I hope everything's in place. I'm going to get there early." She turned to Shannon. "Which is why I'm here. I'm going to scoot out of here, run home and change so I can get back to the restaurant."

"You do that, and quit worrying. I can meet you there and help you out."

"No, no, don't be silly. I'm just a wreck. You know me and events. Take your time getting gorgeous," she said with a wink, then turned to Max. "You should see this dress Shan is going to wear tonight. *Mon dieu* it's something to behold. Fits her like a second skin and really shows off her hot bod."

"Kaitlyn!" Shannon said, feeling the heat tinge her cheeks.

Max turned to her, arching a brow. "Really? I can't wait to see it. Nothing like a beautiful woman in a hot dress."

Kaitlyn laughed. "See? I knew I liked you, Max. See you both later."

After she left, an uncomfortable silence surrounded them. Shannon turned to the papers on the table, neatly stacking them and hoping that Max would just disappear.

"Hot dress, huh?"

She cringed, making a mental note to kill her sister later. "It's just a dress."

"Kaitlyn said it's hot."

"Kaitlyn's trying to act like a matchmaker."

"Really? Now that's interesting."

She glowered at him. "Don't get any ideas. We are *not* a match. My family just has this inherent desire to want to match me up with the first available man that comes along." Hell, for all she knew he wasn't even available.

"Because they care about you and want to see you happy."

Quickly turning away, she concentrated again on the stack of papers. "I can find my own man."

"And have you?"

He'd approached and now stood much too close to her, close enough that his warm breath brushed the hairs at the nape of her neck. She shivered. "Have I what?"

"Found a man."

"That's none of your business."

"That means no."

Gathering the paperwork and binders in her arms, she turned, holding them in front of her chest like a shield of armor. "Stay out of my personal business, Max."

"What if I want to be part of your personal business, Shannon?"

"You can't be."

"Yes, I can be, and I intend to." He leaned casually against the table, reaching out to run his fingertip down her arm. Now she wished she'd worn her suit jacket, because the touch of his skin against hers had her thoughts scattering like leaves on a windswept day.

"I have to go. I'll see you at the cocktail party." She brushed past him and hurried out the door, nearly running down the hall and shutting the door to her office. She dumped the papers on her desk and stepped to the window, watching the people walk by outside.

No, she did not want to have that conversation with Max. She didn't want to know what was on his mind. Hell, she already knew what was on his mind. Same thing that was on hers.

Sex.

If the event tonight wasn't a Storm affair, she'd hide out in her condo in her pajamas and eat potato chips. Avoidance was a good thing, sometimes.

But tonight was a cocktail party that had many functions. And tonight they'd meet with the cream of the crop of New Orleans' society and business. She had to be there.

And so did Max.

Damn. She wondered if she had another dress to wear besides the one Kaitlyn had dubbed as "hot". The last thing she needed tonight was "hot".

Time to bring a fall chill to the air.

* * * * *

Max patiently waited while the elevator took him to the top floor. When he stepped out, he grinned at the name emblazoned over the entry door. The *Lune de l'amour* Restaurant. Moon of love. How fitting. Max opened the door and stepped inside, immediately directed to a private room where a small crowd had already gathered.

Now this place had romance. From the elegant table settings, to the artwork, potted palms and floor to ceiling arched windows, *Lune de l'amour* spoke of elegance and everything that was sensual. Soft lighting cast the room in an amber glow, and live music played in the background. Subtle, but enough to spark his senses and make him wish he and Shannon were going to be here alone tonight.

Ah well, he'd have his chance.

Logan and Aidan were already there, dressed in tuxes, too. They motioned him over and handed him a glass of champagne.

"I hate these kinds of events," Logan mumbled, adjusting his bow-tie. "An evil necessity, but I don't have to like them."

Aidan shrugged. "I just show up, smile, and talk my head off to anyone who will listen."

Logan rolled his eyes. "You're in marketing. That's what you do. At least you have a gorgeous woman on your arm to distract you," he added, inclining his head toward the other end of the room.

Max's eyes widened at Melissa's short, red cocktail dress. Couldn't be described as too much, yet it hugged her curves nicely. Max looked to Aidan and said, "You're a very lucky man."

Aidan grinned and winked at his fiancée. "Don't I know it." Turning to Logan, he said, "If you're lonely for a woman, I could let Mom know when she and Dad show up tonight. I'm sure she'd have a girl for you before the end of the night."

Logan groaned. "I don't need that kind of help. I can get my own woman, thanks."

"Yeah, we all know what kind of women you choose. For someone who takes risks in business, you sure play it safe with women, Logan."

Logan shot a glare at Aidan. "You know why. Let's not talk about this."

Max felt the undercurrents of tension between Aidan and Logan. Logan was holding back...in many areas, the most prominent being the magical powers he possessed. But why? Why wouldn't he embrace them?

"Hey you guys. If you were going to start matchmaking, you should have called me over sooner."

Max turned and smiled at Kaitlyn, looking gorgeous in a long blue dress that showed off voluptuous curves. "Evening. You look beautiful."

She grinned. "Thanks. And busy, too. So what are we talking about?"

"Finding a wife for Logan," Aidan replied.

"Asshole," Logan muttered.

Kaitlyn's eyes widened and a grin curved her generous lips upward. "Oooh now there's a subject I like! If only we could figure out what type of woman Logan liked, then maybe we could find him one."

"I don't like *any* type of woman."

Kaitlyn arched a brow, and Logan rolled his eyes. "You know what I meant, dammit! I'm too busy right now."

"Famous last words. You're lucky I'm busy with this event tonight, or I'd be finding suitable female company for you."

"Then thank God you're busy."

Kaitlyn giggled, kissed Logan on the cheek and waved as she scurried off. She gave off energy vibes like nothing Max had ever experienced. The woman was a dynamo. And yet he sensed underneath that busy exterior lurked a very patient, very warm woman who just needed a man to help settle her down.

Great. Now *he* was matchmaking! Turning his attention back to Logan, he said, "I take it your mother and sisters want you to find a mate."

"It's a never ending parade of contestants," Logan said with a sigh.

"You are getting up there in years." Aidan stabbed Logan's ribs with his elbow.

Ignoring Aidan, Logan grabbed another glass of champagne and downed it in one gulp. Then he turned to Max. "Shannon called me late this afternoon. Said your ideas for national and international exposure are phenomenal."

Max was surprised she'd even mention it, as opposed as she'd been to his ideas a few days ago. "Thanks. Her statewide blitz was damned impressive. She's very good."

"That's why we keep her around," Aidan said with a lopsided grin.

"Holy hell."

Max turned to Logan, who had paled considerably after uttering that oath. He followed Logan's gaze, and his jaw dropped.

Shannon had walked in, wearing what could only be described as a dress that fit her like it was part of her skin. Black, snug, short, with high heels that showed off her long, slender legs. The bottom of the dress skimmed her thighs, flaring out in swirls of near invisible black fabric around the edges. And the top of the damn dress squeezed her breasts together. Max held his breath, expecting them to spill out the top of the dress at any moment.

Thoughts of getting her out of that dress remained prominent on his mind. Hell with getting her out of it. He wanted to lift it up, bend her over the nearest table and fuck her until his driving need for her was satiated.

Her brothers would probably frown on that idea, though.

"Our little sister has certainly grown up," Aidan said.

"No shit. A little too grown up if you ask me."

She spotted them and walked over, her hips swaying gently in a subtly sexy way that had Max wishing he'd worn a longer coat. His cock twitched, coming to life as it sensed her approach. Visions of licking between her breasts had him nearly drooling in anticipation.

Tonight. It had to be tonight. He couldn't wait any longer to mate with her, to make her his.

Smiling at Aidan and Logan, she ignored Max completely. "I see you started the party without me."

"Did you forget something?" Logan asked, glaring at her like a disapproving father.

"No, I don't think so. What did I forget?"

"The other half of your dress," Aidan added before Logan could say the words.

Her cheeks pinkened, but she lifted her chin. "There's nothing wrong with my dress. I'm decent."

"Barely," Aidan mumbled.

"You prance around in that damn napkin-for-a-dress all night, and you're going to end up as the dessert on some dickhead's plate," Logan said with a frown.

Max fought back a grin as he thought of himself as the intended "dickhead". The Storms were a protective pack. He liked that. He had a little sister, too. He knew what they were feeling, because Chantal had grown up way too fast, at least in his eyes. A tiger of a lawyer who'd breezed through college and law school years before others her age, she frequently worked among the ravaging beasts of industry. And he'd never liked the way some of those men leered at her. Fortunately she was good at fending them off. Too good, according to their mother, who wanted her only daughter married off to the "right man".

To him, Chantal would always be a little girl. Even if she was in her mid-twenties now.

Then again, he was leering at Shannon, and his intentions toward her certainly weren't honorable. Talk about wearing two faces. He was quickly becoming the master at it. If Logan and Aidan knew what he was planning to do with their sister, he had a feeling he'd be on the ugly end of a beating.

Shannon put her hands on her hips and glared at Logan. "It is not a napkin. Trust me, everything important is covered."

"Not nearly enough," Aidan added.

"Leave the poor girl alone. She looks fantastic."

"Thanks, Lissa," Shannon said, turning to Melissa and hugging her. When she looked back at the men, her lips turned up in a pout that had Max thinking of blow jobs. Probably wasn't her intent at all.

Melissa sidled up to Aidan and planted a kiss on his lips. "Can I drag you away?"

Aidan wagged his brows. "To some dark corner for a quickie, hopefully?"

Melissa rolled her eyes. "Don Boudreaux of the Chamber wants to speak with you."

"I prefer the dark corner, but okay. Later," he said over his shoulder as he walked away with Melissa.

"And I see someone I need to talk to. Excuse me," Logan said, leaving Max standing alone with Shannon, and utterly unable to breathe. He tried a deep inhale, but only succeeded in picking up her subtle scent. The woman was going to drive him insane if he didn't have her soon.

Her eyes told him that she wanted the same thing. And yet a wariness shadowed her face. That and the cool breeze around them warned him that this wasn't going to be easy.

"You take my breath away, Shannon," he said.

Her cheeks colored a deep pink. "Thank you. You look amazing in a tux," she said, then sucked in her lower lip as if she regretted giving the compliment.

"And you look good enough to eat."

She arched a brow. "Said the wolf to Little Red Riding Hood."

She had no idea how close she'd come to being completely accurate. "Do I look like the big bad wolf?"

Her eyes widened. "Um, no. Not at all. Shall we mingle?"

"How about we dance instead?"

"I don't think so."

He felt the chill in the air, figured it was her magic. She was purposely trying to evade him, but why? Maybe he was getting too close? Or perhaps he was getting under her skin, making her feel off balance.

Good. He liked her that way. Easier to pounce. "Afraid of the big bad wolf, are you?"

"I'm not afraid of anything. We're here for business, Max, not personal pleasure."

"So, you're indicating you could receive personal pleasure from me?"

She huffed out a sigh. "No, that's not what I meant and you know it. Now do you mind? There are a lot of people I want to talk to tonight. Influential people. People who will spread the word about The Rising Storm casino."

"In other words, you don't trust yourself in my arms. You're afraid of me."

Her eyes narrowed, shooting icy daggers at him. Perfect. Why he enjoyed tormenting her, he didn't know. Probably because she provided such a passionate reaction to his teasing. If she didn't care about him, she wouldn't react like she did.

"I'm not the least bit afraid of you."

"Prove it. Dance with me."

"This is ridiculous."

"Coward."

"That's it." She marched onto the makeshift dance floor, then turned and held out her hands. "Okay, Fred Astaire. Show me what you've got."

He intended to.

Chapter Five

ဢ

Did Max have to look so breathtakingly handsome in a tux? Shannon kept as much distance between the two of them as possible, hoping to at least manage to appear cool and calm, though she was anything but.

Damn, he smelled good. And the tux molded itself to his body like it had been sewn on. She found it difficult to resist running her hand over his shoulder, feeling his muscles bunch tight and hard underneath the jacket.

He looked dark, dangerous, like a secret agent.

Or a man with a secret. Something about Max signaled warning bells in her head, but she couldn't put a finger on it.

"I don't have leprosy," he said with a teasing smile, then yanked her flush against him. Her bare thigh brushed his leg.

She swallowed, then looked around, hoping for something or someone to rescue her. Not that he appeared to be willing to let her go. She felt imprisoned, as if she couldn't pull away if she wanted to.

The really bad thing was, she didn't want to.

He shifted, pulling her even closer, if that was possible. "Would you relax? I don't bite."

Ha. That remained to be seen. Or not seen. No. Bad mind, bad. Don't go there.

"Unless you want me to. Do you like a little nibble, say, on the neck or shoulder?"

Her gaze flew to his. Tiny wrinkles crinkled at the corners of his eyes when he flashed that gleaming grin.

"Yes, I see it in your eyes, Shannon. Makes me really curious as to other things you might like."

If she could find her voice, she'd tell him in no uncertain terms that she wasn't the least bit interested in his bites, or anything else he might have in mind. She'd be lying, of course. Visuals entered her mind—being entwined with him and having him sink his teeth into the soft flesh of her shoulder as he rode her hard and deep.

Max inhaled, his eyes drifting closed for a brief second. When he opened them again, the grin had left his face. "I want to make love to you, Shannon. Tonight."

Desire coiled deep in her belly and moved south quickly. Her nipples tightened, her breasts swelling against the material of her dress. Thankfully, he couldn't see.

And how was she supposed to respond? Her mind screamed *no fucking way*, but her body shrieked *Yes! Yes! Oh, hell yes*! "That's not a good idea."

"Fuck 'good idea'. I want you."

Had someone turned the air conditioning off? It was blistering hot. Droplets of perspiration settled between her breasts. Her panties dampened. Had to be the heat.

She had to get her traitorous body under control and quickly. They were in the middle of a cocktail party with hundreds of people around them.

And her legs were trembling.

"Max, let go of me. This isn't going to happen between us. Not tonight, not ever."

"I say it will happen. And it will happen tonight."

His response gave her exactly what she needed. A little righteous indignation to cool her libido. "You're so smug, aren't you? Do you always think you can have whatever you want?"

There was that devastating smile again. "Do you?"

"I control my own destiny, Max. No one tells me what I will or won't do."

"Maybe before you met me. I know you like to be in control, Shannon. I'll bet you even have to tell your men what pleases you in the bedroom. You like to call the shots, tell them when and where."

"Exactly."

"But I'll bet deep down inside, you're hoping that somewhere out there is a man who'll take that control away from you, who'll tell you what to do and when. And who instinctively knows just what you need without having to ask you for directions how to get there. You're begging for it. And I'm going to give it to you, exactly the way you want it, and exactly the way I want it."

No! His egotistical suggestions didn't excite her in the least. In fact, she was just about ready to haul off and slap him one.

"Mind if I cut in?"

Saved by the bell. Or in this case, her mother. Who was, as usual, beautifully attired in a long, golden dress that caught the light and dazzled like sparkling champagne. She kissed her mother on the cheek. "Hi Mom. You look stunning. When did you get here?"

Her mother grinned. "*Merci, ma belle*. You look beautiful, too. We slipped in about five minutes ago. Your father and I have been watching you dance with this handsome man here. Care to introduce us?"

Shannon stepped back and hugged her father, grateful for their timely interruption. "Max Devlin, this is my mother, Angelina and my father, Galen."

Not the least bit wary, Max enthusiastically shook her father's hand, then kissed her mother on both cheeks. "It's a pleasure to meet you both. Your daughter has me so spellbound I didn't notice you standing there. My apologies."

Max sized up Galen immediately. An exchange of something elemental and slightly magical occurred between them, a spark that he felt like a warm air current sizzling through him. An awareness, almost like a meeting between two alphas of opposing packs. He'd seen it before, felt it before. Respected it. Galen Storm was not someone to mess with. Max had sensed the same thing when he first met Logan and Aidan. Without words, he communicated his intent to Galen, showing his respect by stepping away from Shannon, acknowledging that his child didn't belong to Max. Yet.

Galen nodded. "It's a pleasure to meet you, Max. I've heard very good things about you from Melissa."

"Thank you, sir. I'm honored to be working on The Rising Storm's public relations campaign."

"Okay, before you two get involved in business talk, I'd like to dance with this young man here. Galen, dance with your daughter."

"Yes, dear," Galen responded dutifully, winking at Angelina as he led Shannon around the dance floor.

Max pulled Angelina into his arms. Damn, the woman was breathtakingly beautiful, no matter what her age. Petite, her body still that of a young woman's. Glossy, dark hair reflected the light of the chandeliers, curls streaming down the side of her face and resting against prominent cheekbones. Her amber eyes sparkled.

"You're here for more than just The Rising Storm's campaign," she said.

Now how could she know that? Or maybe she was just fishing.

"I'm not sure what you mean, Mrs. Storm."

"Call me Angelina. And I think you know exactly what I mean."

Did he? He knew the Storms had magic, and he could certainly feel a power emanating from this diminutive yet obviously commanding woman. If Shannon had it, then it stood to reason that Angelina had it, too.

"Why don't you tell me what you think you know, and I'll tell you if you're right?"

She laughed, soft and gently. "Oh, you're very good, Max. I can see why Shannon likes you."

"She told you that?" That would be a surprise if it were the case. As it was, he'd been expecting a resounding slap across the face from her before her parents showed up.

"Of course not. I know my daughter. She's very stubborn." Lowering her voice and glancing around the room, she whispered, "She gets that from her father."

Now it was Max's turn to laugh. "I think she might get some of her high spiritedness from her mother, too."

"Maybe. Now as far as what you want, I can sense you're different from most men."

That was an understatement. "Go on."

"And you have an agenda while here. One that goes beyond the campaign for The Rising Storm."

Okay, she was right on that one, too.

"You're very powerful, Max. But keep this in mind. So am I, as is my family. I sense you have an attraction to my daughter, and while I don't necessarily feel that's a bad thing, I won't stand by and watch her be hurt by anyone. We defend our own."

A fierce mother protecting her young. How could Max not respect that? "I understand, Angelina. And believe me, the last thing I want is to hurt Shannon. I believe we share a destiny."

She arched a brow. "A destiny? How so?"

Max wasn't certain how much she'd already guessed about him, so he wasn't going to volunteer too much information. How could he explain to Shannon's mother that he was a werewolf and had chosen her daughter for his mate? She just might not like that idea. "I believe we're fated to be together."

"Interesting you should say that. I felt a connection between you two as soon as I walked in the room tonight."

That knowledge would probably help him later on, provided he needed some Storm family assistance in getting Shannon to see the light.

After they danced, Angelina directed him to several of the key business people in New Orleans and introduced him. She stayed by his side, joined shortly thereafter by Galen. Max spent the better part of an hour with them both, impressed with their business acumen and their inherent ability to make their customers feel like old friends.

For the next several hours he'd met just about every important business contact, and had spent time with both Logan and Aidan, doing a little promotion of the hotel/casino as well as talking about the public relations program.

He liked this family. A lot. They were close knit but friendly enough to open themselves up to a stranger like him. Reminded him a lot of his own family.

During the entire evening, Shannon had kept her distance from him, a fact that apparently was not lost on Angelina as they watched Shannon dancing with her father again.

"She's avoiding you."

"So I see."

"You're not going to let her get away with that, are you?"

"Not very likely. She and I have unfinished business this evening."

Angelina grinned and nodded. "Good. Take me over to my husband."

He swept Angelina in his arms and moved casually toward Galen and Shannon.

"She won't be easy, you know."

Max laughed. "I think I already knew that."

"She's headstrong."

"I like that. But so am I. I want an equal, Angelina, not a meek woman. And Shannon is definitely not meek."

"Agreed. You two will have to fight it out, then. But I feel something deep within you, Max. Something elemental and powerful. You know of our magic, and I know of yours."

Once again, she surprised him. "You know what I am?"

She rolled her eyes. "Of course."

"And you don't object?"

Angelina shook her head. "There are all types of people in the world. Some have no magic within them at all. Then there are others, like you and me, who are different, possessing powers that the average person has no knowledge of. As I told you before, as long as you don't harm my daughter and your intent is honorable, I have no objection to what you are. A merger of Storm and Devlin magic could be very potent."

"That it could." A new admiration for the strength of the Storm family filled Max with hope for the future. He felt a lot less lonely in this strange new place.

"Now I'm going to return you to Shannon, who, by the way, is currently shooting daggers at you. I'm certain she thinks you and I are plotting against her."

"Aren't we?" he replied with a grin, dancing her over to her husband and daughter.

Her eyes widened and she threw her head back and laughed, then patted Max on the cheek. "You're a charmer, Max Devlin."

"And you're a lovely woman, Angelina."

"*Merci*. Ah, there's my gorgeous husband." Angelina moved gracefully from Max's to Galen's arms, then pushed Shannon toward Max. "*Ma belle fille*, go dance with Max so he doesn't feel all alone."

Sauntering quickly away, Angelina and Galen left Shannon standing in front of him.

A very unhappy looking Shannon. She started to turn away, but he caught her wrist and pulled her against his chest, then weaved her into the throng of dancers.

"I don't care to dance any more," she said, gritting her teeth through a smile.

"Oh, but we had just gotten to the good part earlier when we were interrupted by your parents." He spotted the balcony and maneuvered them closer to the double doors.

"You mean the part where I drive my knee up between your legs and crush your balls?"

"Nah, not that part. The part where I sweep you out onto the balcony for a little alone time."

Before she could offer a protest, he had moved through the open balcony doors.

The night was breathtaking, like the woman in his arms. Sultry, steamy, filled with magic and passion. Her hair gleamed in the partial moonlight, her skin taking on a pearl-like glow.

"I'm going back inside." She turned, but he held tight to her wrist.

"Stay here with me."

"We're not here to play, Max. I have work to do." Anger tightened her features. But she didn't tug at his hand again.

"You've worked long enough. Now it's time to relax a bit."

"Does 'no' just not fit into your vocabulary?"

"Not where you're concerned. Besides, you don't really want to say no. You want to say yes, but you're afraid."

She wrenched her arm away and turned toward the balcony, gazing out onto the busy street below. Okay, they were making headway. She hadn't gone inside yet.

"Psychoanalyzing me now?"

"Not at all. I just sense your emotions."

Despite the heat, a cold wind swept over them. Shannon's hair blew back in the stiff breeze, yet she didn't budge nor appear to be cold.

"Don't assume to know how I feel, Max."

Max stood firm despite Shannon's attempt to freeze him. "Let me tell you exactly how you feel, Shannon. You're angry because you can't control me like you've controlled other men in your life. You're angry at yourself because you feel something for me that you don't want to, and it scares you."

When he stepped closer, the wind howled fiercely, the temperature dropping by degrees. She'd put up a barrier, or was trying to. But he'd never been one to let anything keep him from a goal. Undaunted, he stopped behind her, reaching for her arms. Instead of grabbing her, he caressed her from her shoulders to her wrist. She shuddered, but didn't turn around.

"You're wrong. That's not how I feel."

"Deny it all you like, but there's a connection between us."

"That's my mother talking."

"Your mother and I agree, then. There's something that ties us together, Shannon."

"That's all bullshit. Nobody tells me what I should feel or for whom."

"I'm not telling you anything you don't already know. You already feel this way; you're just trying to deny it. I'm curious as to why."

"I don't want you."

He turned her around, trying to be gentle, but his patience was wearing thin. He wanted her. His cock was raging, the primal instinct to mate overpowering his normal common sense. The urge to slam her against the brick wall behind them, lift her skirt and drive his cock in hard and deep grew stronger by the minute. If they didn't leave this party and soon, that's exactly what he would be doing.

Ignoring her denial, he swept his hand over her hair, shuddering at the silken feel of the strands as he threaded his fingers through them. She opened her mouth to speak, but he'd had enough of arguing. Instinct told him to follow through on his deepest desire, and right now his deepest desire was trying her damnedest to get away from him.

That he wouldn't allow, so he followed his instinct. He backed her up against the wall then drove his mouth down over hers, silencing anything she might've said. His tongue invaded, his lips coaxing hers to respond.

He tried to be gentle. God knows, he tried hard, but lust had taken over, the need to possess stronger than the desire to take things slowly.

Expecting a fight, he was surprised when she whimpered and met his thrusting tongue with equal fervor, her body drawing closer to his. He wrapped his arms around her and crushed her to him, her full breasts pressed against his chest.

The wind died down, replaced instead by a simmering heat that made him want to strip them both naked right there on the balcony.

Not a bad idea at that.

No, there were people inside. Passion warred with logic. He had to get them out of there, had to find a way to get off this balcony and head to the hotel.

To his suite, where he could undress her slowly, savor every moment of this first time.

Who was he kidding?

"Aw, fuck it," he grumbled against her lips.

Shannon tore her mouth from his and met his gaze. "My thoughts exactly."

Chapter Six

ஐ

Shannon knew she would regret this later. But later was…later. Right now, all she could think of was Max.

He buried his face in her neck, his tongue licking along the delicate skin. She dug her nails into his shoulder and held him in place, never wanting the delicious sensations to end. His low, guttural growls drove her crazy. Delirious with passion, she didn't even care they were on the balcony and that nearly everyone she knew stood only a few feet inside.

Screw it. She wanted this. Summoning up a blast of wind, she directed it at the doors and they blew closed. For good measure, she summoned another strong gust to scoot the wrought-iron loveseat snug against the doorway.

That should take care of anyone wanting to wander outside. As far as the people below, they'd never see. Shrouded in darkness and tucked against the wall, a large potted palm provided enough coverage to assure them privacy.

Hell, this was New Orleans, and they were smack in the middle of the French Quarter. People wouldn't bat an eyelash at a couple engaged in a little outdoor passion anyway.

Max lifted his head and looked at the door and loveseat, then at her. "You do that?"

"What if I did?"

He grinned, his teeth gleaming bright white against his tan face. "Great idea."

His smile died and he grasped the back of her neck, drawing her mouth to his. He licked her lips, coaxing her mouth open with his tongue, then diving inside.

A mix of emotions clouded her judgment. She shouldn't want this. Impulsive behavior was so unlike her, and yet she felt as if she'd been pulled into a vortex and was powerless to stop the raging storm.

Keeping a tight leash on her powers was going to be difficult if Max continued to sweep his hands possessively over her body. Like a man in desperate search of something, he gripped her arms, his fingers traveling down and over her hips, clenching and unclenching his fingers against her flesh.

When he raised the back of her dress and palmed her buttocks, flames of burning desire licked at her skin He was hot. She was even hotter. And more than ready for whatever he had in mind.

His touch wasn't gentle and exploratory. Barely leashed passion burned inside him, threatening to consume them both.

An insane sense of urgency enveloped her and she knew that sex with Max would be combustible. She prayed for the strength to keep the hurricane at bay.

"Too many clothes," he murmured, bending down to lick the swell of her breasts rising above the top of her dress. She threaded her fingers in his hair and held tight as his tongue snaked into the valley of her cleavage.

With a savage tug he pulled the bodice of the dress down, baring her breasts. He kissed each globe, laving her nipples with his tongue. She sank her teeth into her bottom lip to keep from shrieking as tight pleasure coiled deep within her. He tugged on the aching buds, just as he had in her dream fantasy.

He devoured her breasts, taking as much of them into his mouth as would fit, and wrapping his hand around the rest. Moaning loudly, she closed her eyes tight and just went with the flow of incredible sensations.

When he'd had his fill of tasting her, he dropped to his knees and she opened her eyes, feeling a breeze between her thighs as he lifted her dress.

Max leaned in and pressed his mouth against her panties, his hot breath tantalizing her with the promise of what would come next.

But surely not out here. He wanted to fuck her, that much she knew. But this?

"Max, stop." The words came out like a sensual plea rather than a command to cease. She was powerless against his onslaught, barely able to breathe, let alone carry on a conversation.

"No," he mumbled. "Need to taste you."

"Later."

"Now!"

Her legs shook with the force of her desire as Max spread them apart, then tugged roughly at her panties. The feel of the lacy silk thong scraping her legs was more tantalizing than anything she'd ever experienced. Max helped balance her as she stepped out of them. He tucked the scrap of black fabric into his coat pocket.

The knowledge she was fully naked under her dress, that her breasts were bared to someone who might see, both mortified and aroused her.

But nothing was more enticing than seeing Max on his knees before her, lifting up the hem of her dress and staring at her sex.

When his gaze met hers, his eyes were pools of dark desire, his lashes like the darkest night and those strange yellow flecks in his eyes were glowing.

"I love the way you smell," he whispered. "Like sweet honeysuckle mixed with the unmistakable scent of sex. I'm going to eat you until you scream for me, Shannon. And then I'm going to fuck you until you scream again. And I don't give a damn who hears it."

She shuddered her next breath, unable to respond. Not that he expected her to, because he leaned in and pressed his lips against her clit, then licked her.

Shannon couldn't withhold the gasp that escaped her lips. Nor the whimper that followed when his exquisite tongue traced every contour of her pussy, diving between the folds of her slit to lap up the juices seeping freely there.

This was nothing like what she was used to when it came to sex. Max had been right. She *had* controlled the men she'd been intimate with before. Maybe she'd purposely attracted men she knew she could dominate.

But deep down inside, she'd never been satisfied with a man who took his orders from her. In business, she was in charge. In the bedroom, she wanted a man to master her.

Max Devlin would never be dominated by anyone, man or woman. That she already knew. It was a strange thought to be having while he worshipped between her legs, but even this act showed his control over her, because she was quickly losing any she'd had. Or thought she'd had. She hadn't been able to control a damn thing since the moment she'd met him.

She tangled her fingers into his hair when he lifted one of her legs and placed it over his shoulder, then spread her wider, opening her sex to him. He slipped two fingers inside her wet cunt and thrust hard. Biting down on her lower lip to keep the cries at bay, she panted instead, overcome with sensations of blinding heat and a sweet ache that built fast and furious within her.

He covered her clit with his lips and sucked, drawing out the mewling sounds that couldn't possibly be coming from her throat, nor the guttural groans that made her sound like a desperate bitch in heat.

But damn if he didn't make her want, make her need this magical moment when he completely overpowered her and took her to a place she'd never been.

A part of her fought against giving up that last thread of control. It became a battle then. Her holding back, wanting to prolong the inevitable, and him taking her completely over until she couldn't help but surrender to his special magic.

She felt the tightening, the spiraling between her legs and deep into her core as he fucked her with his fingers, licking the length of her. When he removed one finger from her pussy and slid it gently into her anus, she gave up everything to him.

Despite the fact they were outside where all could hear, despite the fact her entire family lurked mere feet away from them, she screamed as her climax washed over her, trying to keep the wailing cries tucked inside, but unable to do so.

Her powers let loose too, a maelstrom of wind swirling around them, nearly lifting her off the ground.

She fought to manage it all as she rode out the torrential orgasm, finally succeeding in calming the wind as the last of the quakes inside her resided. But she was afraid she couldn't stand on her own.

Fortunately, she didn't have to. Max rose and stared at her. He didn't speak, just gazed at her with eyes that were so hot and filled with desire that she felt the flames lick to life inside her again. She heard the rustling of his zipper, but before she could reach out and grasp his cock he drove into her, thrusting hard and deep in one quick motion.

He was huge. Long and thick, he could barely fit it all inside her. She'd never taken a shaft this big, never thought she could. But her juices poured over them both, her lubrication and prior orgasm allowing him easy access into her willing cunt.

She cried out at the intensely pleasurable sensation of being completely filled.

This time, though, Max covered her cries with his mouth. She tasted her pleasure on his lips and tongue and suckled, taking in his groans with an eagerness that surprised her. When he lifted her and cradled her buttocks in his hands, she wrapped her legs tightly around his waist and held onto his shoulders, not wanting him to pull away from her.

Not yet. Already she felt the tightening, shocked to find that he could bring her so close again, so quickly after she'd just come.

No words were exchanged, only whimpers and moans and a primitive language that had nothing to do with normal speech. Yet she understood Max's desperate need, because she felt it herself, needed him to take her, to come inside her, to brand her as his.

Later, she'd think about the ramifications of what they were doing. Now, she only knew she wanted whatever he gave her, accepting it gladly. If she could find the words, she'd beg him for it.

As long as he didn't let go, he could have whatever he wanted from her.

His thrusts became harder, faster, his cock rubbing against the sensitive nub of her clit and shooting electrical sparks that made her shudder. She felt him reach deep inside her, stroking her high and deep, touching all the parts of her with intense pleasure.

When the exquisite pulses started, he pulled his mouth away and locked his gaze to hers.

"Look at me, Shannon. I want to watch you when you come on my cock."

He moved his hips back, then forward, grinding against her inflamed clit. She wanted to squeeze her eyes shut, this intimacy more than she could bear.

"Look at me, dammit," he said, desperation tingeing his voice.

She did, watching as his eyes began to glow a golden yellow. His jaw was clenched, sweat beading on his brow as he moved furiously within her.

Clenching his arms, she held tight as the first spasms overcame her. Yet she kept her focus on his face, watching his features tighten. He opened his mouth and let out a howl as he shuddered, his hot come shooting high and deep inside her.

She couldn't hold back, her own climax pouring over him, yet he continued to ride her, pushing for more than she was capable of giving.

More than she wanted to give. She couldn't do this, couldn't give up her soul to him.

"Max, please," she begged, knowing what he wanted, and also knowing she couldn't do it. Not again.

"Give it to me again, Shannon," he commanded in a voice that would normally piss her off. But this excited her, this mastery he had over her senses. Relentlessly he moved against her until she felt it build within her once more. Her eyes widened as the shock of realization swept over her.

"I'm coming, Max. Oh, sweet mercy, I'm coming!"

He kissed her, hard, deep, plunging his tongue inside her mouth to match the rhythm of his still-rigid cock. And he came again with her, grinding his mouth against hers until she couldn't tell which of them was groaning.

Breathless, she dropped her head onto his shoulder, trying to calm the frantic beating of her heart. He released his hold on her buttocks and let her legs drift down, keeping his arms around her until he was certain she was steady on her feet.

Yeah, right. Like she'd ever be steady on her feet again after what just happened.

He held her like that for awhile, stroking her back, running his fingers over her skin and pressing light kisses against the top of her head. She wanted to stay in this position forever, without words, without reality creeping in and stealing away what had to have been the best sex she'd ever experienced.

The most emotional sex she'd ever experienced.

Which was precisely why she needed some distance from him. This had been way more than she'd expected and too much to handle.

Now would come the part she hated the most. That awkward, not sure what to say after the sex part.

Already, the realization hit that this had been a huge mistake, that having sex with Max would cause nothing but trouble. She barely knew him, they were supposed to be working together, and the last thing she needed was the constant embarrassment of being reminded what had transpired tonight.

What was even worse, deep inside her lurked the theory that he'd done this, had gotten so close to her, because of some need to wriggle his way into her family, to get close to her brothers, her sisters, and her.

She was certain this whole fucking thing had been business to Max.

Well, she'd played that game before and wasn't going to again. Never would she allow a man to trample her heart on his way to the top.

Trying to be as cool about it as possible, she fixed her dress and her hair, wishing she could summon up a cold bite of air right now to cool her aching flesh. Although she knew she'd just made an error of epic proportions with Max, her body was still flushed with the aftereffects of hot and fiery lovemaking.

No, not lovemaking. Sex. Fucking. That was all it had been.

Too bad it had been with someone she'd never want to be with. Max was too controlling, and she liked to reign over her own world. No, they definitely would never make a viable couple.

"Well, that was fun. Thanks," she said, hoping she came off relaxed and unaffected.

Just treat it as casual sex, and it'll be fine. Close your heart, keep things business-like and cool. Then, maybe it won't hurt.

Max had been adjusting his pants and glanced up, a confused frown on his face. "Huh?"

"I said, this was fun. But I really have to get back inside."

"That's it? It was fun? Thanks for the fuck, gotta be going now?"

She refused to even consider the hurt look on his face. He was just annoyed because he didn't get to say it first. "Um, yeah, that's pretty much it." When he didn't respond, she continued. "Come on, Max. You know as well as I do that this was nothing more than two people with great chemistry who mutually scratched their sexual itch. Now it's over. I hope you don't think I intend to let this affect our business arrangement."

"Business arrangement," he repeated, as if she was speaking some foreign language.

"Yeah. You remember? Business? The reason we're here tonight?"

"I know why we're here tonight. I also know that what just happened was a helluva lot more than a sexual itch. And I think you know that, too."

"Do I? We're adults here, Max. I'm a big girl. Don't feel like you have to bring me flowers or take me to dinner just because you fucked me." She tried for a light laugh, hoping she succeeded. "You were fantastic, really. But I don't need a man in my life. Well, except for the occasional…you know."

"Are you actually buying all this bullshit you're spouting?"

No, but she hoped he would. She blinked, trying to look innocent. "I don't know what you mean."

"I admit that most men would fall for the let's-just-have-sex-but-no-relationship line, and in fact would be grateful for the out. But I'm not that kind of man. We're no way near to being finished, Shannon. In fact, this was just the beginning."

Okay, he may have been a fantastic lover, but really, did his ego have to be as huge as his dick?

"No, Max. We're finished." She turned, intent on making her exit through the doorway, except she forgot that she'd slammed the wrought iron loveseat against the door and couldn't possibly move it without using her powers.

Powers, now that she recalled, Max had clearly seen. And hadn't batted an eyelash over. Well hell, if he wasn't going to ask about them, she sure wasn't going to offer any explanation.

"We're a long way from finished, Shannon." He stepped over and easily moved the loveseat out of the way, opening the door for her. She smoothed her dress, hoping she didn't look near the mess she felt like, and sailed through the doorway.

The evening had been winding down when Max had danced her onto the balcony earlier. Now, it appeared as almost everyone had left, with the exception of her parents and Kaitlyn, Logan, Melissa and Aidan.

They looked at her and she read the knowledge in their eyes. Well she'd be damned if she'd offer any explanation. In fact, let Max explain to her brothers what he'd been doing to her out on the balcony. But she wasn't going to stick around for the inevitable third-degree.

"Night, everyone!" She smiled and waved as she strolled past them, grabbed her bag and walked out the door, desperately hoping that Max wouldn't follow her.

The late-night air had cooled as she walked outside and gave the valet the ticket for her car. Blissfully relieving cool air.

Which swept right up her dress, reminding her that her panties still resided in Max's coat pocket.

Screw it. Let him keep them as a souvenir. She snorted. Yeah, right, like he'd even give a second thought to what they'd just done.

But it had been fabulous. Admittedly, the best sex she'd ever had. And more. But the *more* part was nothing more than a flight of afterglow fancy. There was no connection between them. Never would be. Max was a driven businessman, and she was equally driven.

They'd just be driving in opposite directions.

"Are you all right?"

She whirled around at the sound of her mother's voice.

"Of course I'm all right. It's just been a long day and I'm tired."

"What happened with Max?"

"Nothing." The last person she needed grilling her right now was her mother. "Why aren't you inside giving Max the third degree, instead of me?"

"Max doesn't need to provide this family any explanation. He's talking business with Logan and Aidan right now, and that's all."

Leave it to her mother to tell everyone to mind their own business. "Well, that's fine. I'll get an update from him tomorrow, then."

Her mother lifted a stray curl off Shannon's shoulder and said, "I'd say you got something else from him tonight."

She'd never get used to discussing her sex life with her mother, even if they did have an open communication nearly unheard of in most families. "Really, Mother, I don't want to talk about it."

"He cares for you."

"No he doesn't. He doesn't even know me."

"He knows more about you, about us, than you think."

"What do you mean?" How could he know? Then again, he hadn't blinked twice when she'd summoned the wind to close the door and move the furniture. Most men would probably want an explanation for how that happened. Max hadn't asked.

"He has powers of his own, *ma douce*."

"What kind of powers?"

"That is for you to discover on your own."

Well, hell. Nothing like being completely in the dark about things. Now her mother knew more about Max than she did. "I don't want to know any more about Max Devlin than I already do."

Angelina laid her hand over Shannon's heart. "Your heart and soul speak louder than your denials. You feel something for him."

"I swear if one more person tells me that tonight, I'm going to scream."

"Don't be ridiculous. You can't run from your heart, Shannon. You know that. Give Max a chance."

"No." Where was her damn car, anyway? She did not want to have this conversation with her mother, and absolutely refused to think about Max anymore tonight.

"He is your destiny."

"I'll decide what my destiny is."

"*Mon dieu*, are all my children as thick-headed as their father?"

Shannon laughed at her mother's frustration, and placed a kiss on her cheek. "Probably. I'm sorry, Mama, but I don't buy into that destiny stuff. I make my own choices. Always have, always will. Max doesn't fit into my life. He never will."

Patting her daughter on the cheek, Angelina gave her one of those I-know-something-you-don't-know grins. "We'll see, won't we? Your car is here now. Get some rest. *Je t'aime, ma belle.*"

"*Je t'aime, Mama.*"

After Angelina stepped back inside, Shannon shook her head and headed to her car, more confused than ever.

Try as she might to ignore what happened tonight, her body still burned for Max, her heart squeezing her chest in a funny way that she'd never experienced before.

No. She would not feel for him. She was stronger than her emotions. She'd prove it to herself and to her family that she was going to create her own destiny.

Right now, she needed a bath, a stiff drink, and her bed.

Where, with any luck, she wouldn't be dreaming of Max and wolves.

Chapter Seven

ഗ

"You've been avoiding me. I wanted to talk about the party, but I didn't see you at all Sunday. And today you've been holed up in here with your door closed. What's going on?"

Shannon looked up at Kaitlyn, who leaned casually against the doorway to her office. Damn. She'd managed to avoid her family the entire day. Hell, she'd even managed to steer clear of Max, who fortunately had been busy with Aidan. "I was tired Sunday. I ran some errands, then I went to bed early."

Kaitlyn walked in and sat in the chair across from Shannon's desk. "Tired, or didn't want to talk about what happened with Max?"

"Nothing to tell."

"That's not what I saw. Or felt."

Sometimes having magical family members was a royal pain in the ass. "Butt out, Kait."

Jeweled bells tinkled against Kaitlyn's wrist as she shifted in the chair. "Now, you know me better than that. How can I butt out when I sense something special between you and Max?"

The pounding headache she'd awoken to this morning intensified. She rubbed her temples and glared at her sister. "There's nothing special between Max and me. We had sex. That's it."

Kaitlyn's eyes widened and she leaned closer. "Sex? Really? Out on the balcony?"

"Yes."

"How exciting! And then what happened?"

"Then I went home."

"Shannon!"

"Really, Kait. It was nothing. Obviously, Max and I have chemistry. We had great sex. End of subject."

"So what happens now?"

"Now we get back to work and try to forget what happened." And if she was really lucky, she'd actually be able to do that.

"I don't think it's that easy."

"Sure it is. What? You've never fucked a guy and promptly forgotten about him?"

Kaitlyn stared at her fingers. "No. It's not in my nature to be that callous. And neither are you, despite what you say."

Okay, that one stung. But Shannon and Kaitlyn were different. Like night and day, spring and fall. Where Kaitlyn was warm and nurturing, Shannon preferred to bury anything emotional under layers of cool indifference. Safer that way. "Much easier all around if you'd quit taking these kinds of things so seriously."

"And I think you'd be much happier if you opened your eyes to the possibilities of love."

She tossed her pen on the desk and leaned back in her chair. "I don't love Max Devlin."

"But you could, if you gave him half a chance. I feel it, Shan. And you do too. You're just avoiding the inevitable."

"Now I know how Aidan felt when we ganged up on him about Lissa."

"We were right, weren't we?"

"Yes, but that was different. A blind man could have seen what was between those two."

Kaitlyn nodded. "Exactly. And maybe you should remove those blinders from your own eyes, Shan. Max feels for you. Something deep."

What a load of crap. They barely knew each other. Love at first sight just didn't happen in real life. What Max felt for her was physical attraction, and nothing more. Same thing she felt for him. And now that they'd gotten the sex out of their systems, they could concentrate on business.

"I see fine. I just don't want it."

"And what is it that you don't want?"

Shannon's throat went dry at the sight of Max in her doorway. Lord, he looked delectable in his black suit, white shirt and blue tie. He'd loosened the tie and undid the buttons on his collar. Crisp, dark hairs peeked out from the top of the shirt, making her wonder if his chest was covered in that dark pelt.

Hell, he'd seen plenty of her the other night, while she'd never even glimpsed a portion of his naked body. All she'd had was the feel of his enormous cock pounding her pussy.

Her pulse raced as the images came flooding back to her.

Yeah, she'd forget about him all right. When hell froze over.

Time to cool things down. "What I don't want is to be disturbed."

Undaunted, he walked in and sat in the unoccupied chair. "She always this cranky?" he asked Kaitlyn, pointedly ignoring her.

Kaitlyn grinned. "Frankly, yes. But more so when she doesn't get enough sleep."

"I'm in the room here, guys. Quit talking about me as if I'm invisible."

"Paranoid too, I see," he added.

"Yes. Really pathetic, isn't she? How we'll ever find a man willing to put up with her is beyond me."

"Knock it off, Kait," Shannon warned.

"Would take one helluva man, wouldn't it?" Max winked at Kaitlyn, and she laughed.

"How did the meeting go with Aidan?" Shannon asked, hoping to turn the conversation away from them teasing her.

"Fine. The marketing and PR angles merge perfectly, and I suggested a few things to Aidan and Melissa about taking their marketing to a national and international level. We've got a good start."

"Good. I've got the announcements and community specials set up to go out to all the newspapers this week, plus the regional print publications."

"We're set then. So, what time are you two cutting out of here?"

"I'm finished for the day," Kaitlyn said. "As a matter of fact, I'm outta here. Promised Mom I'd do a little shopping with her today. She's got some ideas about revamping the kitchens at the original Rising Storm, so I'm off."

Shannon knew damn well that Kaitlyn didn't have to rush off. Once again, her manipulative little sister was trying to give her and Max some alone time. As if they needed it. "See ya, Kait."

"Bye Kaitlyn. Say hello to your mother for me," Max said.

"Will do."

After Kaitlyn left, Max turned to her. "Got any plans for tonight?"

"No," she replied, then cringed. What if he asked her to go out with him? Why didn't she say she was busy? Idiot. This is what happened when she didn't engage her brain before her mouth opened.

"I have a line on a house, and wanted someone who lived here to come with me. If you're available, I'd love it if you would come with me to take a look."

"A house?"

"Yeah, you know. Frame structure, some rooms inside, walls, that sort of thing."

She rolled her eyes. "I know what a house is. Why are you renting one?"

"I'm not. I'm going to buy one."

Her headache began to thrum incessantly. "Buy one? Here?"

"Yeah."

"Why?'

"Because I'm moving here."

There was no way he'd said what she thought she heard. Fighting the rising panic, she tried for calm. "You're what?"

"I'm moving to New Orleans. Permanently."

"No you're not."

His lips curled in a smile. "Yes, I am. Do you have a problem with that?"

Hell yeah, she had a problem with it. She stood and paced behind her desk, trying to fathom what that would mean. Max, here in New Orleans, permanently. Oh no, that wouldn't do at all. Much easier to fuck him and forget him if she were actually allowed the opportunity to forget him. Domiciled a thousand or so miles away was a perfect way to get a man out of your thoughts. Out of sight, out of mind, right?

"Why do you want to move here?"

"My family wants to expand the Devlin business ventures nationwide. I'm taking care of the south, and figured New Orleans was as good a place as any to set up shop."

"I've heard Georgia's really nice," she suggested, hoping he'd grab the hint.

He arched a brow. "You're not in Georgia."

"No, of course I'm not. I'm right…what do you mean?"

"It means you're one of the reasons I'm staying."

No. She would absolutely *not* have an emotional reaction to that. "You don't even know me."

He stood and approached her. With each of his steps forward, she took one back until she ran out of space, the back of her legs hitting the credenza.

"I do know you. And you know me. And it scares you."

As if she didn't have her mother and her sister to contend with, now Max was joining the let's-tell-Shannon-how-she-really-feels club. "Save the full-court press for someone who can appreciate it, Max. The only thing you're succeeding in doing right now is pissing me off."

"You want me." He leaned in, his breath caressing her temple. He inhaled swiftly, then let out a whispered sigh.

Her nipples hardened. "Back off, Max. I mean it."

"You mean you haven't thought about the other night at all? Haven't thought about what it felt like to have my hard cock driving in and out of your pussy until you screamed?"

Her body remembered. Despite wanting to forget what happened between them, her body was keenly aware of every touch, every kiss, every thrust of his huge shaft in her cunt. She heated from the inside out, her face flaming in mortification as she realized that he had mesmerized her in some way, had stolen her free will, her right to choose.

"No!" She pushed hard at his chest, using her magic to propel him backward as a gust of wind threw the door back and slammed it against the wall.

Shannon glanced at the door, then back at Max.

He wasn't the least bit concerned over her weather-related tantrum. In fact, his eyes darkened and his wicked smile led her to believe that he was rather turned on by her show of strength.

"You're like some dumb caveman," she said, hoping to irritate him enough that he'd leave. "Are you so thickheaded that you don't realize that I don't want whatever it is that you're selling?"

He shrugged and moved to the doorway, pulling the door away from the wall. "I just asked you to come with me and help me find a place to live. You're the one who got all emotional over it."

"I got…ooooh! You're incredible, you know that?" How could he be so dense?

Leaning against the doorway, he crossed his arms. "Thanks. I was hoping you thought it was as good as I thought it was."

"I'm not talking about sex, you idiot. I'm talking about your balls of steel."

"Aww, shucks, now you're embarrassing me. But thanks."

She stopped, realizing she'd meant to insult him, only it had come out a sexual compliment. "I give up. You win this round. I can't match wits with the witless."

"Whatever you say. Now, will you come and look at the house with me?"

Her first thought was to say no, but he'd probably never leave her alone. She'd go with him, and tell him the house was horrible. "Fine. When?"

"I'll pick you up about six-thirty. I thought we'd grab some dinner and then look the place over."

"Whatever. Six-thirty is fine." She jotted down her address and handed the paper to him. "Now, please, I beg you. Get out of here and let me finish up for the day so I can go home and change."

"Yes, ma'am. You're in charge, ma'am." He winked and walked out.

In charge, her ass. She'd never felt less in charge of anything as she did right now.

* * * * *

Max watched the confusing mix of emotions cross Shannon's face as they ate dinner in an out of the way place that catered to the locals. She frowned, mumbled to herself and shook her head a lot. Rather amusing, actually.

A pile of shredded crawfish shells littered the newspaper tablecloth in front of him. To her credit, Shannon had polished off quite a few, too. Watching her tear into the shellfish with her fingers, then suck the juicy meat out had him eating his own dinner with a raging hard-on.

Butter glistened on her bottom lip, and she swiped her tongue over her mouth to lap it up. Fantasies of her going down on him with such eager zeal only made the torment worse. A sudden need to see her tongue licking up *his* juices had him shifting uncomfortably in his chair.

"Something wrong?" she asked.

Like she'd notice. She'd barely looked at him through dinner. He took a long swallow of beer and shook his head. "No. Food's great."

Grinning, she nodded. "Yeah, I know. This place has the best seafood in town. Nothing fancy, just a great seafood and beer joint."

And the fact she found a place like this so enjoyable told him a lot about her. In Boston, he'd dated a lot of women who were all about society and culture and wouldn't be caught dead in a restaurant with rough-hewn wooden floors and rickety tables that wobbled when you set your glass down.

But he liked the atmosphere. It was noisy, Cajun music filled the room, and families gathered here. He could already envision he and Shannon and her family crowded into one of the long tables in the back of the room. Or even better, he and Shannon and their children.

If someone had told him a year ago that he'd be daydreaming about a mate and pups, he'd have said they were talking about the wrong guy. Because those sure as hell hadn't been in his goals then.

The drive to mate had come upon him suddenly. Surprisingly, right about the time he was invited to New Orleans and began researching the Storm family, specifically Shannon. One look at her and he'd felt a squeezing in his heart. Right then he'd known there was something about her that compelled him.

Now he was looking at buying a house, choosing a mate and settling down to have babies. Good thing his brothers couldn't see him now. They'd laugh their asses off about how the mighty king had fallen.

Well, except for Jason, of course. He'd led them in falling for a woman. A human woman, too. Not lycan. Jason hadn't been remotely ready to settle down, and then suddenly...bam! Out of nowhere he'd shown up in Boston, head over heels in love and his fiancée, Kelsey, in tow. If Jason could do it, he sure as hell could do it, too.

"So, tell me about this house you're thinking of buying," Shannon said, pushing her plate to the side. She took a long swallow of her beer, then wiped her mouth and sat back against the wooden chair.

"I was out for a drive the other day and came across a house right on the lake. Really nice. Lots of land, great looking two-story frame with a huge, wraparound porch, screened and shuttered."

"All the houses are screened and shuttered because of the potential for hurricanes. You know we get those here. Very dangerous. You might want to think twice about settling down here."

He coughed and took a big gulp of his beer to disguise the laughter. When he could speak again, he said, "I'll take my chances."

"The bayou and wetlands are breeding grounds for mosquitoes."

"I like bugs."

"Oh." She went silent then, flicking the empty shells of the crawfish with her fingernail. Then she looked up at him. "I've heard there are wolves in the area. Actually, I've seen them. Scary suckers, too. Very dangerous."

Now he did choke, so hard he was gasping for air and his eyes filled with tears.

"Are you all right?"

"Yes," he wheezed, trying like hell not to fall on the floor laughing.

"Don't you think it might be wise to rent somewhere first, in case your plan to move here permanently doesn't work out? What if you buy a house now, then decide you hate it here? Lots of people hate it here, you know."

From her encouraging look, he got the idea she was hoping it wouldn't work out. Too late. He already knew this was where he belonged. "Not at all. I'm ready to buy. No sense throwing money down the drain on rent when I can get into a buy right away. Then I can concentrate on getting Devlin Public Relations up and running."

"Oh. Well, whatever then."

It was hard not to laugh. Shannon's emotions were so transparent, at least to him. Clearly she wasn't happy he was moving here. That could be both a good and a bad thing. He understood her need to keep her distance. God knows he'd done it himself plenty of times in the past, although not for the same reason. He'd easily kept his emotions at bay because no woman had been able to draw them out of him.

Shannon sure knew how to push his buttons, though. It was true that he didn't know her background in depth, he knew enough just by sensing her emotions. Her distress whenever she was around him meant that she felt something for him, and that was a very good thing.

They drove to the house and waited out front for the realtor, a very enthusiastic woman named Marcy with a lot of blonde hair piled high on her head. After Max convinced her that he really just wanted to walk through the place on his own, she agreed to stand idly by instead of taking him on a room by room tour.

Not like he was going to steal anything since the place was empty. He'd done his homework. He knew the owners had moved out of state over a month ago.

He'd snuck inside a half open window the other night and had a look around, so his decision was already made. What he really wanted to gauge was Shannon's reaction.

She walked through the rooms, her sandals flip-flopping on the wood floors. He admired the womanly curve of her body silhouetted by the dress she wore, a cool blue sundress with tiny straps. He itched to peel those little straps slowly down her arms. Then again, the material was so flimsy it would probably rip easily under his hands.

A hard-on was not a good idea right now. He adjusted the crotch of his jeans and tried to keep his mind focused off the sway of her hips and onto her emotional reactions to the house.

She walked through the entire place and didn't say a word, then waited at the front door.

"Well?" he finally asked.

"Well what?"

"What do you think of the place?"

She shrugged and glanced around. "Too big for just one person."

"Imagine a family here."

She lifted her brows in question. "Family? Is your family moving down here?"

"No. But someday I'll have one of my own."

"Oh."

Silence. He felt a strange rumbling from within her. A quiet unease. Soft, yet stirring him in subtle ways that were inexplicable.

Then she turned to him, narrowed her eyes and placed her hands on her hips. "There's no room for you to do your corporate climbing at The Rising Storm, Max."

"Huh?"

"If your intent is to slide into a partial ownership or takeover of my family's business, you can forget it. My family runs this hotel. Not outsiders."

She'd lost him about two sentences ago. "I have no idea what you're talking about. I'm not interested in The Rising Storm other than as a client."

"Uh huh. I've heard that one before. But suddenly you're really interested in me, then you want to move here. You've got your future all planned out, don't you? Well let me tell you, it won't be at the expense of my family. Go make your fortune elsewhere."

Shocked, he could only stare at her. Then, he threw his head back and laughed out loud. She crossed her arms and tapped her foot.

When he could finally speak again, he said, "I already have."

"What?"

"I said, I already have made my fortune. My family has more money than...well, actually, more than yours. The last thing I need or want is any tie-in financially to your hotel. Relax. I'm not out for your inheritance."

"Then why do you keep pushing to spend time with me?"

Her question shocked him. Surely someone as beautiful and intelligent as Shannon couldn't be that unsure of herself. "Because I like you, Shannon. I want to be with you, not your money, not your family. *You.*"

Her face colored a deep pink. Very cute, actually. She turned and opened the door, mumbling something about needing to get back home because it was late and that she'd wait by the car. He shielded his eyes against the setting sun, chuckling at her obvious embarrassment.

After speaking with Marcy and making plans to put in an offer on the house, he met Shannon at the car and unlocked the door for her.

They drove silently for a few minutes. But he couldn't hold back. "Feel pretty stupid about now, don't you?"

Studying her hands, she said, "I was merely protecting my family."

"I told you I'm not out to hurt your family. You're unbelievable, you know that?"

She half turned in the seat and glared at him. "I have no reason to trust you."

"And I've never given you a damn reason not to. You've got this mindset that I'm out to get you. Tell me, do you treat every man like you treat me?"

"No."

"I don't buy it. I'll bet you don't get many guys warming up to the cold front you put out."

Her eyes widened and she looked away.

"I don't get you, Shannon. One minute you're steaming hot, next you're giving me this great freeze-out for no reason."

"I don't need a reason. I just know men like you."

He made the turn into her condo lot and pulled into a parking spot, then turned off the engine and looked at her. "Men like me?"

Finally, she met his gaze. "Look, Max. We had sex. It was great. How many times do I have to tell you that it's over? Quit stalking me, quit trying to get me to go places with you and quit trying to...to..."

"To what?"

She flicked the lock and threw open the door. "Nothing. Just stay the hell away from me unless it's about work."

With a hard slam of the car door, she walked away.

Dumbfounded, he sat there for a few minutes, having no earthly idea what had just happened.

Shannon was a complete mystery. Hell, maybe it was because she was a woman. The problem was he'd never gotten close enough to one before to get into weird little arguments like this. Maybe he should call his sister. Chantal might be able to give him some insight into the female mind.

Although she'd probably laugh at him. The great playboy Max Devlin, confused about a woman's emotions. Chantal had always accused him of conveniently forgetting that women even *had* emotions.

Well Shannon sure as hell had them. And they were like night and day. Was this normal, or was it just Shannon?

How was he ever going to convince her to become his pack mate when he couldn't figure her out? Normally he was good at reading people's emotions. Okay, maybe not women he dated, but most people he could figure out. Shannon confounded the hell out of him.

Her hard headedness could be a stumbling block. Yes, he wanted a strong mate by his side. She couldn't be alpha female of the pack without having the balls to be in charge. That wasn't a problem with Shannon.

She'd have to learn to bend to his will, and that's where he knew they'd battle. She was not the type of woman to give up control easily. He'd just have to convince her that he was the alpha male of the pack and she'd have to do what he said.

Yeah, right.

Sure as hell figured that the first woman he'd ever wanted to make his mate had to be the one who didn't even want to give him the damn time of day.

Good thing he enjoyed a challenge.

Chapter Eight

ആ

Max was amazed at how much he'd managed to accomplish in a couple weeks. Not only was the PR campaign rolling along, but he'd closed on the house.

He'd spent two weeks making arrangements for his furniture to be shipped down, and his attorney managed a quick closing on the house. Keys in hand, he was ready for move-in day.

Everything was going just as he'd planned, with one exception—Shannon.

During the past two weeks, she'd avoided him as much as possible. Her emotions ran like the finicky fall weather. Steamy one day, chilly the next. It seemed as if she couldn't make up her mind how she wanted to react to him.

But he knew one thing. If he didn't do something and soon, they'd never have a repeat of the "hot" night they'd spent on the balcony at *Lune de l'amour*.. Things between them had been a bit too frosty lately, and he meant to change that.

The urge to mate was foremost on his mind now, and he needed to reveal to her who and what he was. How he was supposed to do that when she wouldn't even talk to him was the problem.

For someone who'd always maintained control of women, Max was damned irritated that he couldn't seem to handle Shannon.

He paced the front of the house while waiting for the moving van to show up, trying to figure out how to finesse his way back into her bed.

Well, hell. For that matter, they'd never ever done it in a bed. Not yet, anyway.

She refused to have dinner with him, had point blank told him that she wouldn't be seeing him socially, and had kept her distance during their business meetings.

Other than a pounce and attack approach, he wasn't sure how he was going to get past the cold shields she'd put up.

Then again, maybe he wouldn't have to, because several cars pulled into the long driveway and stopped in front of him. They were filled with Storm family, from Angelina and Galen to Logan, Kaitlyn, Melissa, Aidan and bringing up the rear, looking reluctant as hell...Shannon.

"What are you all doing here?"

Angelina hugged him and kissed his cheek. "We couldn't let you move in by yourself. What kind of southern hospitality would that be? We've come to help you."

To say he was stunned was an understatement. "I don't know what to say."

Logan smiled. "It's our family's way of welcoming you. When Shannon told us you had bought a place, Mom made arrangements for a moving day barbecue. It's kind of a tradition."

"Don't bother trying to get rid of us," Kaitlyn said as she swept by, arms filled with bags. "We won't listen. You're practically family anyway now that you're moving here. Where's the kitchen?"

Speechless, he mumbled something about through the front door and down the long hallway. The rest of the family followed Kaitlyn inside, Shannon dragging the rear.

"Shannon."

She stopped and turned to him, offering the phoniest bright smile he'd ever seen. "Yes?"

"You've been avoiding me."

"I have not. I've seen you every day at work."

"I'm not talking about work. You've been avoiding me after work." He sounded like a lovesick boy. He was disgusted with himself.

She sighed. "Max, I don't want to get into this again, okay?"

"Why did you even come today if you don't want to be here?"

"I don't know what you mean by that. The Storms are always happy to help."

He wasn't buying it. He could chisel that frozen smile off her face. "Is it that awful to be around me?"

She shrugged. "Again, I have no idea what you mean."

Unable to resist, he reached for her and pulled her against his chest. She stiffened. Anger rose within him at her cold demeanor. He was tiring of these games. He'd given her plenty of space to come around, and was growing weary of tiptoeing around her, around his need for her. "Don't," he warned.

Her eyes widened. "Don't what?"

"Don't pull away from me."

"Then don't touch me unless I invite you to."

"I will be touching you, Shannon. Again and again and again. Might as well get used to the fact that we're fated to be together."

Heat sailed between them like the shock of walking from an air conditioned room to the steamy outside. And just as soon as it hit, it was gone, replaced instead by a gust of cool wind.

Shannon rolled her eyes and pushed hard at his chest. Considering her family lurked right inside, he let go and she stepped back. "Look, Max. Just because we had one night of spontaneous sex doesn't mean you own me."

She was wrong. Mating with her had put his mark on her, at least in his mind. She was his now, and always would be.

He just had to convince her of that, and as usual with Shannon, he was going about things the wrong way. Maybe she just brought out the primitive side of him, and he wanted to possess her. Just take, with or without her permission. And dammit, she *did* want him. He knew she did! She was just too stubborn to realize it.

Jamming his fingers through his hair, he let out a forceful breath. "You're right. Sorry. I'm just...agitated today."

She frowned and tilted her head as if she didn't believe this abrupt change. "I understand. I'm a bit agitated myself."

His agitation was physical. He felt the blood racing through his veins, making him want to shift and take off in a run to pour out some of the adrenaline coursing through him. It was probably because they hadn't made love for two weeks. The anxiety building up within him had nothing to do with this move or with business. It was one hundred percent attributable to the cool brunette standing in front of him. He wanted her, and she wasn't giving him easy access. For a wolf...an alpha wolf...that was damned annoying.

He was just going to have to learn to treat her differently, because his normal alpha tactics weren't going to work on a woman like her. He'd push, and she'd push back. Then she'd distance herself.

No, this way wasn't working at all. Time to regroup and add some finesse to his seduction technique.

"Anyway, I'm sorry. I really appreciate you and your family coming out here to help me today."

Responding with a wary glance, she looked at the moving van coming up the driveway, then nodded. "You're welcome. I'm going inside to help them get started."

Shannon hurried up the porch steps before Max said anything else to her.

She blew a stray hair out of her face and tried to calm her tormented emotions. God, she really didn't want to be here today. He'd bet if she hadn't been browbeaten by her mother, sister and Lissa, she wouldn't have come.

Since the night they'd had dinner and came out here to look the place over, her emotions had been in turmoil.

Hell, she'd purposely picked a fight with him in the car on the way back. And sounded like a bitch royal in the process.

What was wrong with her, anyway? Why couldn't she even be civil with him? He was like itching powder sprinkled all over her body, and he was driving her crazy.

And this damn house didn't help her mental state. She walked through the long hallway in search of her family, once again hit hard with the feeling of home. She'd felt it the minute she'd walked inside that night. It was a beautiful house, but more than that, it seemed to call to her in ways she couldn't fathom.

She pictured her things in this house, her clothes in the closet, her cross-stitched pillows spread across a comfortable sofa. She visualized sitting with Max on a sliding loveseat out on the screened back porch, watching the sun drop down over the lake.

And that made her want to run. Hard, fast and as far away from Max as she could.

When she entered the kitchen, Lissa told her that her mother and Kaitlyn were upstairs getting the bathrooms ready. Lissa was cutting and lining shelf paper in the drawers and cabinets. Shannon worked with her, hoping this day would pass quickly and soon be over.

Max was prominent in her mind. All the time, day and night. Especially night, when he haunted her dreams, a strange mix of man and that crazy wolf she'd seen that one time. Why she continued to dream of the two as one she didn't know, and had given up trying to interpret the images that plagued her.

In her dreams, he made love to her. Savagely, passionately, taking her to heights of earth-shattering ecstasy.

She'd wake drenched in sweat, the remnants of a climax shuddering through her.

It had gotten to the point where she was afraid to sleep. In sleep, Max took over and possessed her, and she gave up control to him without batting an eyelash.

"You're quiet today," Lissa whispered, gently laying a hand on her shoulder.

"I've got a lot on my mind." She cut and fit a piece of drawer liner and slid it in place, grateful for any task to keep her mind occupied.

"Something bothering you?"

"No, not at all." She turned and graced Lissa with a smile. "Although I'd rather be out shopping, or at home reading a book."

"I think you'd rather be avoiding Max."

Now Lissa was getting in on the act? "No, I'm not. I see him every day at work. That's enough for me."

Lissa laughed. "I used to feel the same way about Aidan. That man drove me crazy. Still does," she added with a grinning sigh.

"That's because you're in love. And when you're in love, men drive you to the brink of sanity."

As soon as the words left her mouth, she stilled, knowing she shouldn't have said it.

Lissa's eyes widened. "Maybe you're in love, too?"

"With Max?" She laughed and brushed off Lissa's comment, reaching for more shelf paper. "Hardly. We're more antagonistic toward each other than friendly."

"The night of the cocktail party you were anything but antagonistic."

Oh, shit. Did everyone know what happened between them? Not that they couldn't have figured it out after she'd left the balcony. Her hair had been a mess, her lips swollen from Max's passionate kisses. Hell, her face had beard scratches all over it. She'd looked like she'd been well and thoroughly fucked.

Which she had been. An event her traitorous body refused to forget.

"The night of the cocktail party was a fluke. Honestly, I don't know what happened out there. We were arguing and all of a sudden he kissed me."

"Uh huh. Been there, done that. Some men just get to us. Especially *the* man. The one."

Shannon rolled her eyes. "Ugh. You're spending entirely too much time with Mom."

Lissa laughed. "Maybe. And maybe I just recognize the look now."

"What look?"

"The I'm-falling-in-love-but-don't-want-to look."

If she had that look, then it was a mistake. She wasn't falling in love with Max. Damn her dreams, and damn her interfering family who seemed to think they knew more about how she felt than she did.

How could she be falling in love? She could barely stand him, and obviously he felt the same way since one minute he was nice to her and the next he was yelling at her.

What kind of relationship could they build on something so volatile? They had no foundation. Hell, they didn't even like each other! One push and they'd topple.

No way. She didn't feel anything for Max, and that was that.

Now if she could only stop thinking about him.

* * * * *

Max didn't have a chance to speak with Shannon alone for the remainder of the day. After his furniture had been brought in and placed around the house, the Storms dug right in, helping him open boxes and set everything up.

Then they'd barbecued and eaten out on the back porch, talking, laughing and arguing back and forth.

They were amazing. Rather like his family, a close-knit pack where everyone did their share of the work. The house wasn't huge, but large enough for a couple and growing family, even extra space for visitors. He walked from room to room and imagined a houseful of pups, Shannon running after them. Earlier in the day, he'd stood in the doorway to the master bedroom and watched the movers assemble his king-sized bed, his mind visualizing the set-up and hoping everything would fit. Now, his imagination took a different turn entirely.

Tangled sheets, sweat-soaked bodies and the waning light of sunset filtering through the windows filled his mind with an aching desire to completely possess Shannon.

Unfortunately, that would be hard to accomplish unless he planned to resort to kidnapping.

Maybe he shouldn't hang out in the bedroom right now. He started down the stairs, enjoying the feel of the smooth oak banister under his hand. He could hardly believe it, but the sense of home he felt from this place was comforting.

He liked this house. All wood flooring made the heat a bit less oppressive. There were plenty of screened windows that allowed a breeze to sweep through the downstairs. The living room was plenty big, the white-tiled kitchen enormous.

That's where he found all the women, arguing over placement of dishware. He leaned against the doorway and watched, knowing they hadn't seen him.

"Dishes in the cabinet to the left," Kaitlyn said, drawing a stack of plates and slipping them onto the shelf.

Shannon stopped her. "No, I prefer them on the right. Easier to unload the dishwasher. Plates are heaviest anyway. And the cooking utensils go there, in that drawer," she ordered, pointing to a long drawer next to the stove. "Mixing bowls should go in the cabinets above the island counter, since that's where food would be prepared."

By the time she rattled off her extensive list of what went where, Lissa, Angelina and Kaitlyn had stopped and crossed their arms, staring at her. It took her a few minutes to notice.

"What?"

"You're acting as if this is your house, and you're deciding where everything goes," Kaitlyn said.

Angelina nodded. "You feel at home here, *ma belle*. It's obvious."

Their comments mirrored his thoughts. Shannon had been ordering them around as if she were setting up her own kitchen. Max's heart slammed against his chest at the realization of how much he really wanted her in his home.

Shannon threw up her hands and shook her head. "That's ridiculous. I'm just trying to help out. And I do not feel at home here! I didn't even want to come." She pointed her finger at her mother. "You made me."

Max put his hand over his mouth to stifle the laughter that threatened to spill.

"I don't recall having to twist your arm. Really, Shannon, you're acting like a petulant child. It's obvious to everyone that you have feelings for Max, and you're fighting them."

Now it was getting good. And he had a ringside seat.

"Yeah, and you're getting pretty damn cranky about it, too," Kaitlyn chimed in. "Living with you has been like two weeks with a woman with PMS *and* on a diet. Lord, you've been a bitch."

"Have not."

"Have too."

Angelina rolled her eyes. "How old are you, girls? Really. Shannon, you might as well face your destiny. You know it is inevitable."

"I will do no such thing. I can't believe the three of you are ganging up on me like this! I was merely unloading these boxes, and suddenly you have me married off to a man that, frankly, I can't stand!"

"Methinks thou dost protest too much," Kaitlyn said, a smug smile on her face.

"Don't you go quoting Shakespeare to me. You should get busy finding your own man instead of trying to match everyone else up, or you'll end up alone."

Kaitlyn lifted her chin and sniffed. "It's not my time yet."

"Well, make it your time. Mother, I love you. Kaitlyn, you're a pain in the ass. Lissa, mind your own business. I've had enough of this." She tossed a roll of paper onto the counter and whirled around, storming through the kitchen.

She skidded to an abrupt halt as she rounded the corner to find Max in the doorway. Her eyes widened, then narrowed.

Oops.

"Great. Just fucking great. Get out of my way!" Pushing him aside, she went out the back door, letting it slam behind her.

Max craned his head around the corner to find the three women staring at him. He walked in and leaned against the counter, trying for a look of chagrin. "Sorry," he shrugged. "I eavesdropped."

Angelina arched a brow and crossed her arms. "Didn't your mother teach you it's impolite to eavesdrop?"

"She tried. Obviously, I didn't listen. But yeah, she'd smack me in the back of the head if she'd caught me doing it."

Angelina's stern look turned into a smile, then a giggle. "I like your mother already."

"She'd like you, too. You're very much alike in a lot of ways."

"You miss your family," Kaitlyn said, reaching across the counter for Max's hand.

"Yeah, I really do."

"Then why move here?"

"Because it's his destiny to be here," Angelina said.

"I know that feeling," Lissa chimed in.

"I don't know about destiny, I just know it's something I have to do. Besides, I'm plenty old enough to live away from home and survive." He winked at Kaitlyn, who smiled brightly.

"Good. I'd hate to worry about you getting all homesick on us." Pushing away from the counter, Kaitlyn said, "I think I'll go see what everyone else is up to."

"I'll go with you," Lissa said.

He watched them leave, then turned his attention to Angelina. "Let me put that stuff away. You have all done enough today."

"Just about finished here anyway, and it was no trouble. I enjoyed it. We all did. You're like a member of our family."

"I'm hoping I will be some day." There, he'd put it out there. Might as well see how Angelina reacted.

She paused and leaned against the sink, her arms crossed. "Are you in love with my daughter?"

Love? What did love have to do with any of this? This was about primal urges, about the need to choose a mate. Wolves didn't love. He didn't love. "I want her."

She arched a brow. "Well, at least you're honest about your feelings. But wanting someone and loving them enough to spend the rest of your life with them are two different things, Max. I know Shannon. She won't settle for less than your heart."

He reached inside the box nearest him and unwrapped some glasses, placing them in the cabinet. This conversation had suddenly grown uncomfortable. Lying to Angelina about his feelings for Shannon wouldn't have been appropriate, though, even if it would have been more convenient to just say he loved her.

"Right now, your daughter can't stand the sight of me. So I'm pretty sure she doesn't love me, either."

"Maybe. Maybe not. But if you're not open to the possibility of love, it might pass you by. Are you willing to gamble on losing Shannon because you can't feel enough for her?"

"Angelina, I feel a lot for her. I just don't know yet if it's love."

She took the glassware from his hands and set it on the counter, then grasped his fingers in hers. "Fair enough. I feel what's in your heart. I'm not a mind reader, and neither are my children. Shannon can read your emotions unless you're very good at masking them. Sending her mixed signals will only make her back away from you. If you want her, you need to let her know in no uncertain terms how much."

He started to speak, intending to tell her that he wanted Shannon more than he'd ever wanted another woman, but she stopped him. "I don't mean just physically, although that's important, too. But you'll have to give up your heart to win her, Max. You'll have to do something monumental, something that will prove to her that she's the only woman for you. Otherwise, you don't stand a chance."

Moving away, he scrubbed his hand over the back of his neck and shook his head. "I won't tell her something I don't feel."

"Good. Because that girl has the best bullshit meter I've ever seen. She only wants your honesty. If you can give her that, it's a good enough start."

"I'll do that."

"Now, I think it's time I round up my family and leave you and Shannon alone." She turned and headed for the hallway, but then stopped and looked at him. "Max, remember what I said. I know you're very powerful. So am I. Don't hurt her."

He knew she'd back up what she said. "You have my word."

After she left, he stayed in the kitchen as the parade of Storms came by and wished him well. Shannon stayed outside, no doubt completely unaware that her family had abandoned her, leaving her alone with him.

He glanced out the back door and saw her at the water's edge, sitting on the dock and wiggling her feet in the water. The orange sun had begun to dip toward the trees, bathing her in its glow. Long shadows signaling the coming fall season drifted toward her from the overhanging trees.

Soon it would be dark. He looked up at the sky, not yet seeing the silvery orb, but instinctively knowing what kind of night it would be. He felt it surging within him, the call to turn, to run free, to find others like himself.

Or to make one like him.

It was time to set thing straight between him and Shannon. Time to lay it on the line and tell her his thoughts and feelings. One way or another, their futures would be decided tonight.

Tonight was the full moon.

Determination firmly in place, he headed to the refrigerator, thankful he'd had that appliance delivered early. Grabbing a bottle of wine and a couple glasses, he filled a basket with cheese and slices of French bread.

He opened the back door and stepped out on the porch, a mix of certainty and uncertainty racing through his mind and heart.

Did he love her? Was he even capable of it? He was a cold, calculating, unemotional bastard in business. Arrogant, self-assured and damned successful.

With women, though, he'd never had to prove himself. They flocked to him like moths to the only light for miles. Not once had he given his heart. It had never been necessary.

Maybe it would be, this time. Shannon infuriated him. She was bossy, as arrogant in her business demeanor as he, and as alpha a female as he'd ever met.

She was his match in more ways than just sexually.

Sucking in a deep breath of courage, he pushed the screen door open and went to her.

Chapter Nine

ဢ

Clouds gathered overhead and the wind shifted, coming in off the water. Shannon felt the change in the weather deep inside her, as she always did when her season came about.

Sometimes she wondered if the elements reflected her moods. Other than the ones she conjured up, of course. But sometimes the overall weather patterns in the fall seemed to come from within her. She'd asked her mother about that once, but had only been given a vague "it depends" as an answer.

She splashed water onto her legs, cooling her sun-heated skin, content to just sit here and brood.

Something would happen soon. Something major. If she had a better handle on her emotions, she'd be able to get a clearer picture of what was on the way, but she was too mixed up right now to discern what it was that unsettled her—the weather or her feelings about Max.

Try as she might, she couldn't put that needed distance between them. And because she'd been so damn stubborn, all it did was cause friction between them. Maybe it was time that she just played out this game with him and see where it led.

Down the road to disaster, no doubt. She'd walked that road before with a man she'd been highly attracted to, and what she'd felt for him was nowhere near the jumbled sensations that electrified her whenever she was around Max. Given that even being near him threw her emotions in a state of chaos, giving in to her feelings and attraction for him couldn't lead anywhere good.

And yet, she couldn't seem to separate from him. God knows she'd tried like hell the past couple weeks, to no avail. Even when he wasn't physically present, she felt him. His earthy scent clung to her clothes and on her pillow when she laid down at night. Ridiculous, since he'd never been in her room. They had some weird psychic bond that defied explanation.

Hell, considering her own inherent magic, who was she to deny that mystical forces surrounded them? Look at what she was capable of, and she thought herself an ordinary person.

Maybe Max possessed some type of powers, and she was drawn to that part of him.

"Thinking?"

She shrieked at the unexpected sound of Max's voice. She hadn't even heard him come down the dock. Laying her palm against her breast to calm her speeding heart, she said, "You scared the shit out of me."

He squatted down next to her. "Sorry. You were deep in thought and obviously didn't hear me. What are you doing?"

"Thinking."

"About?"

"Stuff." *Like you. And me. And us. And this infernal battle waging war in my brain right now.*

"Want to talk about it?"

"Not really."

He shifted and sat, resting on his left arm. Shannon took in the sight of him, admiring the way his jeans fit snug against his powerful thighs, the way his T-shirt hugged his chest. Damn he had broad shoulders, too. If she'd bothered to pay attention she'd have noticed that, but she was so busy picking the right words of denial out of her mind that she hadn't focused on the gorgeous man who sat next to her now.

"I brought us a snack." He reached behind him and pulled out a basket containing a bottle of white wine and two glasses, a wedge of cheese and some bread. "Thought we'd have a little picnic and talk. If that's all right."

She frowned and looked toward the house. "Where's my family?"

"They left."

She sniffed, more than a little bit irritated at the oh-so-obvious setup. "Still doing a bit of matchmaking, aren't they?"

"Apparently." He smiled. She'd never noticed his dimples before on both his cheeks, so close to his curving mouth. A sudden desire to press her lips to one of those indentation made her lean back a bit, still unsure of where she wanted to go with all this.

Max poured the wine and handed her a glass. He sliced a thin wedge of cheese and lifted his fingers to her mouth.

She hesitated, the act seemingly so familiar. Still unsure how intimate she wanted to get with Max, she reached for the cheese, intending to feed herself.

But Max snatched it out of her reach. "Uh uh. Let me."

Warily, she opened her mouth and he slid the cheese inside, his fingers lingering as she closed her lips over the slice of brie. She shuddered at the taste of fine cheese and the equally exotic flavor of Max's finger.

He popped a slice into his own mouth and washed it down with a swallow of wine. She watched the movement of his throat as he swallowed, then took a long drink of her wine to escape the sudden dryness in her mouth.

When he lifted a piece of bread toward her mouth, she shook her head. "I can feed myself, Max."

The gold and green in his eyes danced like the flickering rays of sun filtering through the trees. "I know you can. This way is more fun."

She didn't disagree with that, and allowed him to continue to feed her. A simple act, and yet so incredibly erotic that she wanted to try it out herself. She reached for a small wedge of cheese on the plate and lifted it to his lips.

One corner of his mouth curled in a wry grin, and he opened, letting her slide the cheese onto his waiting tongue. Before she could snatch her fingers out, he captured her wrist and held it in place, then closed his lips around her fingers, sucking them into the moist heat of his mouth.

Desire shot between her legs. Her panties dampened and the very air around them seemed to still and warm. When he slowly pulled her fingers from between his lips, she knew what it must feel like for a man to sink into heat like that.

Damn near burned her alive, and that was just the play of his mouth on her fingers.

Their gazes caught and held as Max leaned in. The musky scent that she attributed to him mixed with the wine tingeing his breath. A heady combination that she found near impossible to resist.

But resist she would. At least for the moment. For someone who'd always been self-assured, she sure as hell felt torn between her desires and her common sense right now. And she didn't know which one was the right one to follow. "I haven't seen the inside of the house since it's been set up. How about a tour?"

Max paused, then tilted his head to the side, studying her. She turned away from his intense scrutiny to watch the last of the sun flitting behind the trees.

"Okay, let's go," he said.

He stood, picked up the basket and held out his hand to her, keeping his fingers entwined with hers as they walked into the house.

She kind of liked the feel of her small hand in his much larger one.

When they got inside the kitchen, he set the basket on the counter and turned to her. "Let's take that tour."

He led her through the expansive kitchen and into a formal dining room that stood empty.

"I lived in an apartment, so the set in the kitchen nook was all I had. No reason to have anything formal."

She smiled at his explanation, imagining his bachelor pad back in Boston.

The furniture in the living room was lovely, though. Instead of manly leather, as most single men possessed, a warm beige sofa and matching loveseat graced the living area. Two high-backed Queen Anne chairs in a beautiful pattern of golden browns and rust complimented the couch, along with a few impressive antique end tables and a coffee table. A heavily scrolled pattern etched the rounded feet of the mahogany tables. They were breathtaking and obviously well preserved.

"My grandmother's tables," he murmured, stopping at the doorway leading to the front hall. "My mother insisted that each of us had some of Grams' furniture, and I always liked those pieces."

"They're lovely."

"Thanks."

He waited while she approached the stairs, letting her walk up ahead of him. She was conscious of his eyes on her as she made the trek up the stairs, making her want to rush her pace, but she forced herself to take normal steps. She waited for him at the top, conscious of the way his gaze traveled over her as he made the last few steps.

There were four bedrooms upstairs, and two full baths. She remembered the night she'd come in here with Max, and had fallen in love with the bath in the master bedroom. Gorgeous creamy marbleized tile, with a double vanity, a sunken whirlpool tub and a shower that several people could fit into made it every woman's dream bathroom.

"I won't be using two of the bedrooms...yet," he said as he led her down the hall. "One I've converted to my office since I do a lot of work at home, and until I get a main PR office in town somewhere, I'll just set up here."

She nodded, admiring the enthusiasm in his voice. Maybe she was wrong about his motives for moving here. If she'd bothered to think about him as a businessman instead of just a guy trying to reach the top of the Storm dynasty by way of getting into her pants, then she'd have realized this sooner.

And she'd accused *him* of having a huge ego? Hers was boundless. She'd thought he was really trying to get to her family's money through her, when he didn't need it at all.

But that only left one reason he had been trying to get close to her since the day that they met. He wanted her. Just her. She found it less uncomfortable to think he was just after her money.

"I think I like this room the best," he said, drawing her out of her musings by leading her into the master bedroom.

Wow. Her gaze immediately went to the sliding glass door, which led out to an expansive balcony that overlooked the lake. A king size bed centered the long wall, decorated by a gray and cream bedspread in a satiny finish. Wide, thick pillows were piled on the bed. It was beautiful, but not garish. Inviting, warm, and sensual. "You could fit ten people on that bed!"

"Two would be just fine," he said with a wink.

She swallowed past the nervous lump in her throat, although for the life of her she had no idea what she was nervous about. Yes, she felt something happening between them, but it wasn't like they'd never had sex before. After all, the balcony episode remained first and foremost on her mind every single day.

This felt different. More important, somehow, but she didn't know why.

Quit second guessing things and just go with it! Geez, woman, have you ever had a spontaneous moment in your entire life? Does everything have to be about control?

"Come out here with me. I want to show you something."

She jumped at the feel of Max's hand sliding into hers, yet she allowed him to lead her out the sliding door and onto the balcony.

Her first whiff of the crisp air brought about a sensation of a brewing storm. Max had put some white wicker chairs on the oversized balcony, and even one of those chairs-for-two that slid back and forth like a rocker. Small tables were set next to each chair.

"It's lovely," she said, stepping to the wood railing and leaning over, letting the wind whip strands of her hair from her ponytail. She closed her eyes and let the elements surround her, praying that the cooling breeze would extinguish the fire burning inside her.

"Would you like a drink? I can go downstairs and get the wine."

Did she want to prolong the inevitable? She was at the now-or-never point, the place where she firmly denied him forever, or took a giant leap.

Honestly, she didn't know what to do. Instinctively, she knew that she'd have to give up some control to make love with Max. He wasn't like the men she usually chose. There wasn't a sit-and-obey bone in his entire body.

Maybe that's what really scared her about him. The fact that she couldn't call the shots, that he stirred some need within her that she never even knew she possessed.

The need to be dominated, to give up her control to one person and one person only. Denial had kept that part of her safely buried for years, but now she dragged it out and faced it.

Dare she allow Max to explore that aspect of her? And what would happen if she gave it up to him? Would she ever be able to get it back? Would they ever return to equal footing?

"We seem to find ourselves on balconies a lot," he said, moving behind her and whispering in her ear. His deep voice made her shiver, made her want things she wasn't sure she should want.

"Yes, we do."

Heat simmered between them, around them, mixing with the furious wind that stung her cheeks.

"Weather's getting bad. You want to go inside?"

She shook her head. "No. I love this. It's so primal, like communing with nature. Lame, I know, but I love stormy weather."

His low, husky laugh rumbled against her back as he reached for her shoulders and pulled her against him. "It's not lame at all. I love being outdoors no matter the weather. It's like I'm a part of the elements."

Max was the first man who truly understood how she felt. That was scary enough, let alone her body's reaction to being near him.

He moved his hands up and down her arms, causing goose bumps to pop out on her skin.

"I'm going to touch your body, Shannon. Everywhere. I'm going to undress you out here, and I'm going to make love to you tonight."

There was no question in his rough, insistent voice. He hadn't asked. He'd told her what he was going to do. She opened her mouth to shout a vehement denial at not being given a choice, then closed it abruptly.

Wasn't this what she wanted? To be taken, to give up the need to dominate every situation?

Instead of her natural inclination to argue the point, she remained silent.

She'd made her choice.

* * * * *

Max waited for the inevitable denial to break from Shannon's lips, but she didn't say a word. He'd felt her tense when he told her what he was going to do to her, but it was imperative that she understand how things were going to unfold between them. He couldn't form a mate-bond with her unless she accepted that he was the prime alpha of the pack.

Shit. She didn't even know about him yet. By rights, he should explain to her who and what he was, and what his intentions were toward her. But he'd just gotten her to a point of calm acceptance. Riling her up now would only delay something they both needed desperately.

The sun had fully set, and in its place the moon climbed above the trees, a silvery ball so intense it hurt his eyes to look at it. He drew his power from the moon, and when it was full, he was at his most potent. Primal urges took over then. Urges that he had a difficult time controlling. Most often it didn't matter. He could run them out, and if he wanted to fight there were always wolves around to engage in some rough play. But this was different. This was Shannon, who remained in the dark about what he was. He'd have to fight the pull of the moon, the primal desire to take without asking, to force her, if necessary.

As a wolf, his prime objective was to mate and impregnate the alpha female. He cringed at the thought of possibly doing that to Shannon when she didn't really understand the implications of the act.

It wouldn't be fair to burden her with a lifelong commitment to him if she wasn't given the choice. But his body wasn't interested in fairness right now, and it seemed to want to be in charge. Just standing this close to her was a lesson in patience. He wanted to shred her clothes, bend her over and impale her cunt with his cock. Arousal spread hot and heavy in his groin, hardening him and tightening his balls.

Her scent hung thick and heavy in his nostrils, despite the swirling wind around them. He laid his lips over her neck and drew in a breath of her sweet, musky smell.

The perfume of her desire, the scent of her aroused sex, oozed from her pores. She was primed and ready for his invasion.

The less civilized part of him threatened to surface and take what he'd already claimed as his. He fought back the primitive urges, determined to take things as slowly as possible for her. There would be time enough for savage passion later. Now, he wanted to savor every taste, every sigh, every moan drawn from her lips.

But when she sighed and finally relaxed against him, signaling her surrender to his control, he was hard pressed to keep the wolf within him at bay. The full moon and the desperate need to mate caused the change to begin. Tonight would be a constant struggle between the wolf and the man.

"Shannon," he breathed, taking a long swipe of her neck with his tongue. His blood burned, his skin on fire as the physiological changes swept through him.

No! He wouldn't allow it, not yet.

She reached up and clasped the back of his neck with the palm of her hand, arching her back and thrusting her breasts forward. Unable to resist, he slid his hands over her hips and along her ribcage, lifting the tank top over her belly, exposing her silken flesh.

What a flimsy excuse for a bra she wore. He hadn't expected to find the lacy black bra underneath a casual top. He cupped his hands over the silken lace, flicking his thumbs across the thin fabric. Her nipples hardened to sharp points, her breasts swelling to fill his eager hands.

A gasp tore from her lips as he brushed his fingers over the thin fabric. Desperate for the feel of her bare skin, he grasped the center of the bra and ripped it in half, greedily capturing her breasts. She moaned when his fingers found her swollen nipples, the encouraging sound causing his cock to swell and grow. He rolled the hard tips of her nipples between his thumb and forefinger, rewarded with her sharp cries of delight.

Her whimpers only drove his lust higher, forcing him to concentrate on remaining human. Once the beast within him surfaced, there'd be no turning back. His cock pressed painfully against his jeans, demanding to be embedded in the source of the musky heat surrounding them.

Regretfully, Max released Shannon's breasts, slowly moving his hands down her ribcage and stomach until he found the button on her shorts. He popped it with his thumb, then drew the zipper down, pushing the impeding garment over her hips and toward the floor.

A tiny black scrap of material that he supposed one could call panties covered her mound, with two little strings resting on her hips.

Piece of cake. He reached for the sides and ripped them. A giggle escaped her lips, followed by a pant of pleasure as he drew the remnants of the garment away from her pussy.

He stood back and lifted the tank top off, then turned her around, positioning her so that the full moonlight bathed her naked body.

That first night on the balcony at the restaurant, he'd been more interested in sinking inside her welcoming cunt than doing much gazing. Tonight, he wanted to see her, to touch her skin and taste every inch of it.

"You're beautiful," he said, reaching behind her head to pull the clasp holding her hair up. Waves of silken sable fell over her shoulders and across her breasts. Turquoise eyes darkened as she kept her gaze focused on him.

"This isn't fair," she whispered, her voice filled with husky desire.

"What isn't?"

"I want to see your body. I saw nothing of you that first night. Tonight, I want to see you naked."

His heart slammed against his ribs. He only hoped that the body he presented her with could stay human through all this. Mentally tamping down the wild, raging beast within, he pulled off his T-shirt and slipped out of his jeans, then stood for her inspection. His cock sprang forward as if calling out to her.

Shannon looked down and her eyes widened as they centered on his shaft. "Wow," she whispered, almost as if she hadn't expected him to hear.

But he had, and felt a pride he'd never felt before. This was his woman, and she approved of him. He took a step forward and pulled her into his arms, no longer able to stem the savage flow of desire for her. She came willingly into his arms and wound hers around his neck, pulling his face toward her parted lips.

His mouth came crashing down over hers, his tongue plunging between her open lips. She met his thrust by tangling her tongue around his and rocking her hips against his cock.

A sudden gust of wind shot around them, first hot, then blissfully cooling. Dark clouds sailed overhead, obliterating the light of the full moon entirely. Thunder cracked in the distance. Loud, ominous, the next clap closer than the one before.

Shannon tore her mouth away from his, her luminous eyes searching his face. "I...I can't help it," she cried, digging her nails into the skin of his shoulders.

He wanted to throw his head back and howl at the feel of her possessing him. He held back, instead sweeping his hand over her windswept hair and tracing the upper swells of her breasts with his other hand. "Don't try to control it, Shannon. Let it run free. Let it go."

She stilled and started to pull away, but he wrapped his arms around her.

"I can't do this, it's too much." She pushed against his chest with the palms of her hand, but she was nowhere near a match for his strength.

"You can. You will. I want all of this." He looked to the sky where lightning arced as bright as the moon's glow, then met her concerned gaze.

It was the lack of control she feared, not the elements. He knew it, he felt her hesitation. He also felt a great need within her to let go of that control.

"Shannon," he said, tipping her chin and keeping her focused on his face. "Give it to me."

Chapter Ten

ɕↄ

Shannon met the determined glint in Max's golden eyes. Her fear warred with the greatest desire she'd ever felt.

Max was everything she *never* wanted — controlling and dominant. She knew if she gave it up now, she'd never get it back.

The problem was, with every caress, every kiss, she became less and less interested in keeping control over any aspect of her life.

She sure as hell wasn't controlling the elements right now. From the dark skies to the blistering winds, she knew what was coming, and yet was powerless to stop it. Not now, not when she'd come this far.

For being one of the most momentous decisions of her life, the words slipped out easily. "Take it."

A low growl escaped Max's throat as he bent to her lips. He devoured her, body and soul, in a way she'd never expected to want. Now she not only wanted it, she needed it. Desperately.

He swept her into his arms and stepped through the doorway. Max left the door open and the whipping winds followed them inside, cooling the humid room. With one jerking motion, he yanked the spread off the bed and deposited her on the cool sheets.

Instead of climbing in the bed with her, he stood next to it, watching her. She marveled at his chiseled body, muscular in all the right places. A fine pelt of dark hair covered his chest, a nest of curls surrounding his magnificent cock.

She rolled to her side, at eye level with his shaft. Then she smiled and turned her gaze back to his, asking the silent question, but she already knew what his answer would be.

Max inhaled sharply, then circled his fingers around his cock, and leaned toward her. "Suck me."

His command sparked spasms deep inside her pussy. She felt the moisture seep from her as she contemplated taking his huge tool in her mouth, knowing that soon it would be in her pussy. Filling her, taking her once again to those glorious heights where nothing else mattered but the two of them.

She flipped onto her back and scooted to the edge of the bed, letting her head tilt backward against the edge of the mattress. The position placed her mouth close to the engorged head of his cock. Looking up, she waited, her mouth open and her tongue darting out to lick her bottom lip.

One corner of Max's lips curled into a wicked smile as he stroked his shaft slowly, then leaned in and fed it to her, inch by inch. The tip was buttery soft and she enveloped it with her lips, her tongue swirling over it to taste the sweet drops of pre-come. She surged forward, taking more of him, then moved back, letting it slide partially out.

No way could she get the whole thing inside, but Max kept hold of the base of his shaft and pumped it between her lips. Her pussy ached as she tasted him, pleasured him, rewarded with his groans of pleasure.

He threw his head back and shuddered as she reached for the twin sacs dangling underneath his shaft, cupping and caressing them as she sucked as much of him as she could. Then he leaned forward and rested one hand near her hips, the other sliding between her legs.

Instinctively she spread her thighs wider to give him access. His fingers probed her sex, dipping into her moisture and then moving upward toward her clit. She moaned against his shaft as he circled the distended nub, then rubbed it between his fingers. Sparks of intense pleasure nearly shot her off the bed and her body broke out in a sweat.

She called forth the wind and rain, knowing its intensity could be dangerous, but she didn't care. She was on fire, in desperate need of cooling relief. Lightning shot into the room and arced across the ceiling as if frozen in time. Then a burst of rain showered over them, soaking them both.

She tensed, waiting for Max's reaction. He looked down at her then laughed hard, shaking his head like a wet dog and spraying even more water over them. It wasn't until this moment that she realized how much it meant to her that he accepted her magic, that he didn't look at her like a bizarre mutant or someone to be feared. She'd always worried about her powers, though she didn't fight them as much as Logan did. Still, having Max's approval meant everything to her right now.

He plunged his fingers inside her, dipping slowly and easily until she was going crazy with the need to fucked. Relentless, he maintained gentle strokes, dipping into her pussy and then petting her clit until she wanted to scream at him to fuck her hard and fast. She whimpered, already near a climax.

Quickly, he pulled his fingers out and moved away, removing his shaft from her lips. "Get up and turn around. I want you on your hands and knees."

Heat burst low in her belly. She sat up and turned, facing the wall on all fours, and waited. Max pressed his thighs against the side of the bed and pulled her hips toward him. His cock probed between her legs, the shaft rubbing against her aching pussy.

"Tell me how you want it," he said, his voice strained with a need she understood all too well.

"Hard. Fast and hard."

His nails dug into her hips as he settled against her. With one quick thrust, he embedded his cock deep, giving her exactly what she'd asked for.

Max held tight to Shannon's hips, afraid of so many things he could barely concentrate. The tightly leashed control he had over the wolf was slipping, quickly being replaced by a primal urge to fuck her as the beast he was, to mate with her in his natural form.

But he couldn't, wouldn't, until she became one with him. He'd have to tell her, but later. Not now, not when his seed hovered tight and ready inside his straining balls, eager to spurt forth within her in the hopes of creating life. He pulled back and slammed hard against her, propelling her forward on the rain-slicked mattress.

The room was a mess, the covers soaked and flying around the room as a maelstrom of wind, lightning and rain poured over them. He reveled in the elements, knowing they were Shannon's passion, her desire for him pouring out of her being. And he meant to give her the greatest pleasure she'd ever received.

He slid his fingers against her pussy, drawing away the copious juices of her desire. Spreading her nectar over the puckered rosette bared between her buttocks, he gently probed her entrance, rewarded with a grunt of pleasure and a shriek as he slipped one finger inside her.

Fucking her this way was driving him mad with animal lust. But dammit, he was stronger than the wolf, capable of maintaining control just this once. For Shannon, to make it good for her. To give her what he'd needed to give her since the first moment he'd laid eyes on her picture in the magazine.

With equal fervor he moved his cock in and out of her pussy, watching her moisture cling to his shaft when he withdrew. He fucked her ass with his finger, embedding it deep inside her tight cavern as he once again thrust hard into her cunt.

"Max, please," she cried, bucking against him like a wild beast, crying out his name and uttering begging whimpers. She tightened and pulsed around him and he knew it wouldn't be long now.

"Shh, pet, I know what you need. You want to come."

"Yes," she whispered, her voice low, tense, her back arching as she fucked him back as hard as he was giving it to her. "Make me come, Max. Make me scream."

The control burst and he let the beast loose as he neared the end, feeling the boiling, burning pain of the change. He'd let it half out, and that was all he'd allow right now. Shannon wouldn't see, she wouldn't know. He'd control enough of it that she'd never know the difference.

His nails drew out into claws, fur popping up on his hands and forearms. His teeth lengthened, his facial structure changing as his nose and jaw elongated. He let out a fierce growl as Shannon's pussy squeezed his cock tight, then thrust against her until she cried with pleasure.

Shannon clawed at the mattress as she lifted her ass higher, allowing him to penetrate her deeper with both his cock and his finger. He felt the contractions around his shaft as the first waves of her orgasm overtook her.

A keening wail rent the storm-laden air as she climaxed hard and fast, soaking his cock with her juices and squeezing him in her vise-like grip until he couldn't help but let go. He held his palms over her, refusing to mar her skin with the beast's claws as he growled, leaned over her and sank his teeth into her shoulder as gently as he could, shuddering as his seed shot deep inside her.

The spasms within her cunt had no more subsided than the force of his pummeling orgasm sent her over the edge again. She screamed and bucked up, but he held her in place with his teeth as he rode out the thundering orgasm.

He waited for her to finish, waited until she crumpled face down on the mattress, before he let her go. Panting for breath, he sheathed the beast within himself once again, then collapsed next to her, pulling her against him.

He held her, stroked her hair and her skin, watching the way the soaked strands of her hair quickly dried, as did the bed and the room as the storm withdrew. The wind and rain still lashed against the trees outside, the balcony soaked from the downpour, but the bedroom returned to normal, as if not even a drop of rain had fallen inside the house.

Amazing magic.

Amazing woman.

He could only hope she could accept who and what he was as easily, because he'd have to tell her.

Soon.

* * * * *

Shannon didn't remember falling asleep, but she must have. For how long, she didn't know. The room was still dark, the storm still raging outside.

They should leave, as close to the water as they were. But she didn't have the strength to even lift her head and suggest it to Max.

His body pressed firmly against her back, one leg slung over her hip, one hand wrapped around her breast.

Possessive sort, wasn't he? Although she had to admit, she kind of liked it. The men she'd been with before had all been the gee-that-was-great-gotta-go-now types. No cuddling, no after-sex conversation. She couldn't remember ever having anyone spend the night.

Before, that kind of man had worked fine for her because she hadn't wanted them to hang around after sex, anyway.

Now? Now, she was happy to have slept in Max's arms.

She sighed, truly contented for the first time.

Damn, their sex had been wild. Animalistic, filled with a passion she hadn't known existed. She'd never come like that, one right after the other, and with such an intensity that she'd hovered on the edge of consciousness.

Max had truly dominated her in every sense of the word, pawing her to hold her in place, even digging his teeth between her shoulder and neck.

Like an animal. She shuddered and her tired, sore body flared to life at the thought of him doing it again. Exactly the same way.

She shifted, her buttocks rubbing against his cock.

His very hard cock.

She smiled into the darkness, feeling very much the powerful woman for giving him an erection by doing nothing more than cuddling next to him.

Then again, he might just have to pee.

She giggled.

"What's so funny?" Max asked in a groggy voice, then pushed against her again.

"Nothing. I was just wondering if you were hard because you wanted me or because you needed to pee."

He chuckled. "I did that an hour ago."

"You did?"

"Yeah. You're comatose when you sleep, did you know that?"

"Obviously not." She moved to get up, but his hand snaked out and grabbed onto her hip, pulling her tight against his raging hard-on.

"Don't move."

She waited for irritation to surface. Instead, her pussy dampened and excitement filled her.

Surprise of all surprises. She enjoyed having him control her.

In the bedroom, that is. Outside the bedroom, they damn well better be equals or all bets were off.

"Unless you have some immediate need to get out of bed, and I mean immediate, I don't want you to get up."

She shifted, wriggling her ass against his shaft. "I'm not going anywhere."

"Good." He flipped her over on her side so that she faced him, his face nearly unrecognizable in the darkness. Sliding his hand under her leg, he lifted it over his hip, aligning his cock at the entrance of her pussy.

Shannon wound her free arm around his neck and pulled his head closer, licking his bottom lip. "You taste good. Like a midnight snack."

"Mmm, that's about the right time of night, I think."

"How do you know? There's no clock in here."

He fit his lips against hers and teased her mouth. "I can tell. Trust me."

She'd have to, since she had no idea. Frankly, she wasn't sure she cared. They'd made love, they slept, and from the feel of his hard cock probing insistently against her slit, they'd be doing it again very shortly.

Winding her hair around his fingers, he tugged gently, enough to send sparks of pleasure spiraling down her spine. She turned her head, then winced at the slightly tender spot on her shoulder.

"What's wrong?" he asked, going completely still.

"You bit me," she teased. "It's sore there."

"Where?"

"Right here." She pointed to the spot.

"Aww, baby I'm sorry. Let me kiss it."

He leaned up and licked the tender spot on her shoulder. She laughed then held on as he nibbled lightly down her neck and collarbone. He stopped at her breast, taking her nipple between his teeth and tugging lightly.

Pleasurable pain shot deep inside her.

"Tyrant," she murmured, but she wasn't really complaining. Not when he drew her nipple into his mouth and suckled her.

"Sissy," he mumbled against her breast.

When he moved down and licked the underside of her ribs, she giggled.

"Ticklish, are you?"

"No. I'm not." He moved his hands over her ribcage and tickled her. She laughed out loud.

"Ah, you *are* ticklish."

"No! And stop that, you big bully." She pushed at him, but he rolled her onto her back and pinned her arms above her head.

"You like me bullying you," he argued, nudging her legs apart with his knee and settling between them.

Maybe she did. But she wasn't about to admit it. She'd already given up enough.

"You like me fucking you, too." His voice dropped down an octave, a heated, dark tone that matched the moon-filtered rainy skies. Probing between her legs, he fit the head of his cock between her pussy lips and surged forward, just enough to slip part way inside her.

A soft moan escaped her lips and she lifted her hips to encourage a driving thrust. "Well, yes, I do like that a lot."

"Show me how much you like it." He leaned back, withdrawing his cock until just the head was inside her.

That wouldn't do at all. With determined fervor, she wrapped her legs around his hips and soared upward, grabbing his cock with her pussy. Thunder rumbled outside the screen door, a quick flash of lightning shooting across the sky.

Max let out a grunt of pleasure and dropped her back down on the mattress, driving deep inside her at the same moment he took her lips in a punishing kiss that she welcomed with enthusiasm.

His passion was boundless, and matched her own. This is what she had been missing. How could she ever have lived without this all-consuming need that she knew instinctively could only come with Max?

He buried his head in her neck, kissing and nibbling her throat until she broke out in chills. Slipping his hands under her buttocks, he ground against her sex, his pubic mound rubbing against her clit.

"Max," she groaned, knowing she was close.

"Yes," he hissed through clenched teeth. "Come for me, Shannon."

As if her body obeyed his command, her orgasm rushed through her like a flood, sweeping her away in a high tide of sensation so overwhelming that she tried to escape by pushing at his shoulders. She felt water rush around them, fierce waves lapping over the bed and knew that she'd brought the flood inside the room but was powerless to stop it.

"More!" he shouted, clasping her tighter against him and stroking incessantly until tears came to her eyes. This was too much sensation, and it wouldn't stop as wave after wave crashed through her.

Tears streamed down her face as she went from one peak to another, Max holding her close and murmuring words that she couldn't understand. Her pussy squeezed his cock tight and he tensed, then growled as he jettisoned a stream of come deep inside her. She screamed as huge waves pummeled them both.

He began to jerk against her repeatedly, groaning and licking at her neck and shoulders. She shuddered against him as emotion poured between them, drenching her in sensations that she wasn't sure she could handle.

The water receded slowly, disappearing and drying the room as it had earlier. Her powers once again safely tucked away, she relaxed her tensed muscles.

Shannon blinked away the tears, shocked at what she'd just experienced with Max. She didn't know how to interpret the overwhelming emotions she had when she was with him. Truly, this was unfamiliar territory and it scared the hell out of her. She'd have to back away from this a bit until she found her bearings.

Max rolled off and lay on his back, pulling Shannon against his chest. She rested her head on his shoulder, still breathing heavily and awed at what had transpired.

She'd often dreamed of a man who could take her places she'd never been before. Of what it would feel like when she found that one man who was her match.

She'd found him, all right. She was in love with Max. Infuriating, obstinate, alpha-male Max Devlin was the man who'd captured her heart.

Now what the hell was she supposed to do? He didn't love her. He wanted her, that much was certain, but passion eventually withered. What foundation would they have to build upon then?

Max swept the moist tendrils of her hair away from her face. "Now. How soon can you get your things together and move in with me?"

Chapter Eleven

ஐ

Shannon stilled, not sure she'd heard Max correctly. "What?"

"You're moving in here with me. As soon as you can. There's plenty of space for some of your furniture if you'd like. And the closet in here can more than adequately handle your clothes and mine."

She pushed away from him and sat up, wishing she could see his face in the darkness, certain he was teasing her. "Are you insane? I'm not moving in here with you."

He caressed her back and she shivered, refusing to allow his touch to sway her.

"You and I are destined to be together, Shannon. It's pointless to deny it. You felt what's between us as well as I did. Quit fighting the inevitable."

She wrenched away from his touch and moved to the side of the bed, switching on the lamp. Max squinted against the light.

"What's wrong?" He lifted up on one elbow to reach for her.

She kept her distance. "What's wrong? This is wrong. You and I are wrong. I can't believe you'd be so egotistical as to assume I'd move in with you just because you gave me a good fuck."

He frowned and shook his head. "That's not what this is about. There's a lot more to it."

"I don't care what's going on in your mind. Your suggestion is ridiculous." What the hell *was* he thinking? He'd never even told her he loved her, that he cared for her. Did he think she'd just give up her life and shack up with him so his fucking partner would be close by when the urge hit?

"If you think about it, if you feel it, it's not ridiculous at all. We're mated, Shannon. As sure as if we'd married. You want me. I sure as hell want you. We can start by moving in together, but in short order I want to get married."

Chills crept through the languorous warmth she'd felt earlier. Marriage? Now he was talking marriage? This was all too much. She slipped off the bed and went looking for her clothes, finding them draped over a chaise. The underwear was ruined, but at least she had her shorts and tank top to slip on.

"What are you doing?"

"I'm going home."

"You *are* home." His voice lowered and she looked over at him, shaking her head.

"No. This is not my home."

"It will be soon enough."

He really expected her to move in with him, just because he deemed them a match? And what about love? Was he going to mention the words? Did he even feel the emotion?

Hurt etched its way deep into her heart. Pain that came from the realization she'd fallen in love with the wrong man. A man who wanted to control her completely, not just in the bedroom. One who obviously didn't love her enough to ask her what she wanted, and then let her make her own choices. A man who hadn't even said he cared for her.

"Shannon, it's storming outside. Really bad. Where do you think you're going?"

"I told you. I'm going home."

"You don't have a ride."

She zipped up her shorts and met his concerned gaze. "I'll get a ride home."

He pushed away from the mattress and got up. She couldn't help but admire his long, lean body, the way his muscles bunched along his arms and shoulders.

"You're being unreasonable about this. I'm going to take a shower, then we'll go downstairs and fix something to eat, and talk about it. I have some things to tell you. Important things."

She stood there as he went into the bathroom and turned on the shower. Grabbing her tennis shoes, she hurried downstairs, determined not to be there when he got out.

Tree limbs lashed against the roof, the wind picking up force. How was she going to get out of here in this storm? It was way too far to walk home, and the thought of facing any one of her family members right now made her nauseous.

Dammit, now what? She wasn't going to ask Max to take her home; she couldn't handle having to endure the confines of the car with him. He'd just try to convince her that his way was the right way, and the ensuing argument would be more than her blooming headache could handle.

What she needed was to get away from him and fast.

She went to the kitchen and grabbed the phone, intending to call Kaitlyn. There was no dial tone. Maybe it wasn't turned on yet, or maybe it was the storm. She found her purse and grabbed her cell phone. No service. *Shit*!

Closing her eyes, she willed her magic to come forth, to settle the raging weather outside long enough for her to walk to the end of the road, where she knew a convenience store could be found. She'd call from there. Less embarrassment that way. She could even take a taxi, then she wouldn't have to explain to her family why she was sneaking away from Max's in the middle of the night.

That's what she'd do. But she had to get out of here first. No way would Max wait around while a taxi showed up at the house.

The weather fought her, the storm railing against her powers, but she was stronger. This was her season, these were her elements, and if she wanted it badly enough, they'd obey. They had to.

In short order the wind died down, the rain stopped. Ominous, black clouds hung low overhead, but the fury that threatened to rage was at bay—at least for the moment. She couldn't hold it back forever, but she could long enough to reach the outskirts of town and grab a ride.

Slipping out the front door, she peered around her, wishing for that full moon to light her way, but knew the clouds would not relent. She headed down the long driveway, carefully watching her step. Limbs had fallen in the storm, littering the road like an obstacle course.

The roadway was pitch black, but she'd been this way before and knew where she was going. She pushed back the fear of walking down a deserted road in the middle of the night, rationalizing that no one would be out in weather like this. No one sane, anyway, she thought with a laugh. She'd be fine. No harm would come to her.

She'd made it about a quarter of a mile when she heard a low rumble, looking to the sky to see if the storm was about to break free.

The rumble turned into a growl, and she realized then that it wasn't coming from the sky. It came from the line of trees along the side of the road, deep into the heavily forested bayou.

Shannon stopped, wondering what it could be that made a sound like that. Maybe it was a lost, angry dog, frightened by the storm. That had to be it. She listened for a full minute, and when she didn't hear it again figured the animal had wandered off. She started to move again, but hadn't made it more than a few steps when she heard the growl behind her this time.

Panic caused her throat to go dry, her heart ramming against her chest. She turned slowly, hoping it was a friendly but frightened dog. She loved animals. She could handle this.

But no dog had glowing yellow eyes, eyes that pierced the blackness of the road.

That was no dog. It was a wolf.

Wolves again. Just like the one she'd seen at her condo. Hell, they were out in the middle of nowhere, too. It wasn't unlikely that she'd find all kinds of strange creatures out here, but she sure as hell had never seen a wolf before in these parts. Not even in the rural area where her parents lived.

She summoned her magic, thinking a shot of lightning or a strong hurricane force wind would either scare it into running off or push it away.

Lightning arced down from the skies a mere foot in front of the wolf. It started and backed up a step, then sniffed the air around it and continued to glare at her. She tried the wind, summoning up a gale force at the animal, but it seemed to dig its long claws into the side of the road and held on, its fur blowing back as the gust blew hard against it.

What the hell; were these creatures impervious to nature's elements?

She had two choices. Stand there and let it attack her, or run. If she ran down the road, she was an easy target. If she headed into the trees, she might have a chance at escape, or at least could double her way back to Max's place, providing there was a path to follow.

Deciding anything was better than allowing the wolf to tear her to pieces, she slowly moved toward the trees. The wolf growled, but didn't advance. As soon as she lost sight of it, she broke into a run.

Her shoes immediately sank into the mud, her progress impeded by fallen limbs and watery muck. She heard the growls behind her and to the side, realizing then that there was more than one wolf out there.

Rampant fear cut off her breathing. She wanted to stop, to curl up into a ball and hide from the creatures out there. But she couldn't, had to keep moving or they'd be upon her. She made sure to swerve back and forth instead of running in a straight line, but frankly she had no idea where she was headed. The trees were thick, there were no paths and there sure as hell was no light.

Climb a tree. That's what she'd do. She'd be safe up there because wolves couldn't climb trees. Could they? Hell, she didn't know. She stopped at one she thought had a low enough branch, but her shoes were covered in slick mud up to her ankles and she couldn't get a foothold. The bark was slick on one, and when she tried another, the trunk wasn't stable enough to hold her. Dammit, she didn't have time to try and climb every goddamn tree in the woods!

She fumbled in the darkness, tripping over limbs and rocks, the dense trees and bushes scraping her arms and legs as she pushed by them. She knew she bled, felt the scratches like needle sticks in her skin, but kept moving, hoping like hell she wouldn't run straight into a bayou.

Maybe the water would keep them away. Did wolves fear water? She didn't know, and wished right now that she'd spent more time watching those nature shows on television.

A burning pain seared her chest as she struggled for breath, panic quickly overtaking her. The wolves were gaining, although she had a gut feeling they could have jumped her by now if they'd wanted to. Didn't they run faster than humans or something? It wasn't like she was sprinting at top speed here. Were they toying with her? Was this some kind of game to wear her out and make her an easier target when they tired of chasing her?

Thoughts of Max entered her mind. How close was the house? She couldn't see a damn thing in the darkness, spotted no lights to guide her way. Where was he? Did he know she was gone yet? Would he come searching for her?

Oh, God. If he did, he'd drive down the road, never thinking she'd entered the forested area. Why would she? He'd think she meant to go home. He'd figure exactly what her plan had been and would drive to the store to look for her. How stupid was she? So desperate to escape him, she'd foolishly set out on foot in an area unfamiliar to her. She deserved her fate.

A sick feeling of impending doom swept over her, and she fought the tears that welled and spilled over her cheeks. She didn't want to die out here. Not like this. Not torn apart by these savage creatures.

Max, where are you? I need you. Help me!

* * * * *

Max slipped on a pair of shorts and went in search of Shannon. Maybe she'd gone downstairs to fix something to eat.

Knowing her, she was pissed off and pacing in the kitchen, waiting for him to come down so she could lay into him for suggesting she move in with him.

Okay, maybe he'd blurted. Not his smoothest move, that was for sure.

He had to calm her down, make her see reason.

It was time to tell her everything, explain why she had to be with him. He ran his fingers through his still-damp hair, damning himself for being so caveman-like in telling her how things were going to be between them, instead of discussing who and what he was, then asking her to move in.

Me big, strong man. Me tell woman what to do. Fucking Neanderthal.

He groaned and stepped into the dark kitchen, realizing immediately that something was up.

And that something was not good.

Sniffing the air, he smelled danger, knew instinctively that Shannon was no longer on the premises. The hair on his arms and legs stood on end, and chills popped goose bumps on his skin.

Shannon was in trouble. Big trouble.

He picked up her scent immediately. Not just hers, either, but others, and in close proximity.

Wolves.

"Shit!" He tore out the back door and into the woods, ignoring the burning pain of his body changing as he made the dash across the lawn. By the time he reached the woods, he was fully wolf and ripping through the trees and bushes, hoping he wasn't going to be too late.

It was easy to track Shannon. He could pick up her scent from miles away. He also knew she was panicked, afraid, and quickly running out of energy.

Not that it mattered. They stalked her slowly, enjoying the game. He knew their kind, toying with humans, making a game of terrorizing them, getting off on their fear.

He also knew they wanted her because they smelled him on her, recognized what he was and weren't happy about a new alpha in their midst. They wanted to take her, to put their mark on her, to claim her.

Over his dead body. No fucking way would any of them lay a paw on her.

Granted, this wasn't the way he'd wanted to draw them out of hiding. Not using Shannon as prey. Because he knew they didn't care what happened to her. The only reason they were doing this is because they knew if she was in danger he'd come running, and they thought they could beat him down this way.

Max didn't know who the members of this pack were, but he'd bet they'd never met a Devlin wolf before.

This was his territory now, and Shannon was his mate. He'd take on a dozen of them if need be. When he was finished, they'd know a new alpha was in town, and meant to take over.

She hadn't gone far, thankfully. He stopped about twenty yards in front of her and let out a howl, announcing his arrival to the others. He sensed their fury, their blood thirst, but he felt no fear for himself, only for Shannon.

Now that he spotted her, he felt a measure of relief. She was cut and bloody, but it looked more like branches had done the damage. The wolves hadn't touched her. They could have torn her to pieces in seconds, but they hadn't. He might let them live because of that.

He'd been aching for a fight for a long time, and as he scented their locations, knew this one would be bloody.

He welcomed it. They'd crossed the line when they targeted his woman. He'd either take over the pack or kill them all. Either way, he knew who'd come out the winner tonight.

* * * * *

Shannon stopped and leaned over, resting her hands on her knees, not caring if they attacked her or not. She couldn't breathe. The run, along with fighting her ever-increasing fear, had stolen every ounce of energy she possessed. Her adrenaline rush had passed and right now she just wanted to lie down.

But she couldn't. She leaned halfway up, resting her hand against the bark of a tree for support. The incessant growling grew louder, and she felt a calm peacefulness overcome her, as if she finally accepted her fate.

There was no way she could get out of the woods. But she refused to stand there and let them take her. She'd die, but she'd die running for freedom.

But then she heard a sound ahead of her now, as angry a growl as she'd heard before. Coming toward her, slowly. The sound grew louder and she stilled, praying for invisibility but knowing that it wouldn't matter. They scented her. That much she knew. Wolves hearing and scent were heightened, much more so than a human.

So she waited, watching its glowing eyes as it appeared before her. She met its gaze head on, refusing to look away, refusing to show weakness.

The wolf stopped in front of her. She was sweating now, her body drenched, her heart slamming against her ribs, her legs trembling from fear and exhaustion.

She could barely stand as it stopped a mere inches from her, its teeth bared, a low growl rumbling in its throat.

Lord it was a beautiful animal, though. Even though she feared it, she admired its strength, the gray and white fur that covered strong legs and body. And it was much bigger than she'd ever known wolves to be.

Then it shocked the hell out her. It winked. She blinked, surely delusional in her panicked state. But when it walked around her and behind her, she didn't know what to think. Why hadn't it attacked her?

Slowly, she turned to follow it, her heart lodging in her throat as she realized that at least six wolves were behind her in a semi-circle.

The gray one that had winked stood in front of them, snarling, saliva dripping from between its teeth. She backed away and stood to the side of all of them, not enough that they thought she'd run because one of the six watched her.

It seemed as if the big gray was communicating in some way to the others, because after it growled, the others did too.

She was afraid to move at all, but took small steps backward, sensing that something was about to happen between the gray wolf and the other, darker ones.

The gray took a few steps forward, ignoring the warning snarls of the others, and entered their circle. The strange thing was, she felt concern for the gray. Maybe because it hadn't attacked her. Stupid, she knew, but she really didn't know what to think about what was happening right now. She should take the opportunity to run, but with so many wolves around her, she was afraid if she moved, one would pounce on her. So she stayed put and watched.

They circled each other, moving counter-clockwise, their glowing golden eyes the only thing moving in the dark woods. The six wolves advanced slowly, closing the circle and drawing nearer to the gray.

Shannon shrieked and jumped back when the gray leaped on the center wolves. Then they all fell on him, snarling and growling as the battle ensued.

The tangle of fur on fur made it impossible to determine what was happening. She wished for the clouds to dissipate so she could see how the gray was faring, but it was all she could do to hold back the fierce storm.

They were all engaged. She should turn and run, head back to the road and return to Max's. Anywhere but here.

But her feet were frozen to the ground. She couldn't make them move, couldn't turn her eyes away from the carnage in front of her. Whimpering yelps emitted from the center of the fray, but she didn't know which wolf or how many of them were injured. The growls grew louder, more fierce, splitting the air with the angry sounds of their battle. And all the while she watched. Stupidly stood there and watched.

Suddenly, two of the dark wolves retreated, hovering outside the center of the circle. Soon, two more retreated, and then the other two. They stayed in the circle, moving around the gray, still baring their now bloodstained teeth, still emitting low rumbles from their throats.

They all wore marks, all of them bloody, including the gray, who looked as if he'd taken the brunt of the fight. His fur was torn away in spots, angry bloodstained gouges in his skin.

But the six retreated, their ears back, their tails between their legs.

The gray was the only one left. He lifted his snout to the air and howled, the sound echoing through the near-silent woods.

He turned to her, his fangs gleaming in the darkness, dripping with the blood of the others. As he advanced toward her, Shannon realized at that moment that she should have run when she had the chance.

Now that he'd driven the others off, he was coming for her.

Chapter Twelve

ജ

Shannon held her breath as the wolf limped toward her, its beautiful fur a bloody, matted mess.

But she was certain he could still easily tear her apart. Oh, why hadn't she run when she'd had the chance? What in the world possessed her to stick around? Why had she stood there immobile as if she *felt* like she needed to stay?

Then again, for some strange reason, this wolf had saved her life. She knew it to be so, despite everything she knew about wild creatures. He'd have had no reason to spare her, in fact should have joined with the others in stalking her, but he hadn't. He'd approached, if she could believe her eyes—winked—then walked around her to attack the other wolves.

Maybe that's why she stayed. Maybe there was something different about this one.

The wolf stopped, no more than a foot from where she stood. He raised his head, looking at her, his eyes filled with pain, mouth open as it panted heavily.

She tensed, poised to once again take off in a run if the wolf leaped at her. She might not get far, but it was better than just standing around like a target.

But he didn't advance. Instead, he settled slowly to the ground, laid his head down and closed his eyes.

Oh, God. Was he dead? Still too afraid to get close to him, she watched and waited, mentally counting the minutes until she got to about ten. The wolf hadn't budged, his breathing ragged as he slept.

Now. Take a step backward, then another, and get the hell out of there now! Whether it was fear or some strange compassion she felt for this lethal creature, she couldn't. He was too big for her to drag him to the house. If she could even find the house. As it was she was close to passing out, the fear and her injuries from running through the woods taking their toll on her. At the moment she wanted nothing more than to drop to the ground and close her eyes. Exhaustion made her weave on her feet.

But if the wolf woke, then what? Would he lunge for her? Was he just resting, assuming she'd still be there when he woke?

This was ridiculous. *Run!* She heard the warning in her head and took a tentative step backward, her feet crunching on a tree limb. The wolf woke, lifted his head up, and snarled at her. She froze to the spot, fearful of moving so much as an inch. She reached behind her and found the trunk of a tree, grabbing onto it for support, afraid she'd fall forward right on top of the wolf.

As it was, even if she ran she wasn't sure she could get very far. The wolf, satisfied that she wasn't moving, laid his head back down and closed his eyes.

Too tired to contemplate escape, she gave up the fight, convinced on some level that this creature would not harm her. She scooted down against the trunk of the tree, mindful of the wolf's eyes opening and watching her warily, but he emitted no growl, even when she sat and straightened her legs, putting them precariously close to his jaws.

Sitting was heaven, her battered, stressed body and mind needing desperately to shut down for at least a few minutes. That's what she'd do. She'd rest, just for a few minutes, until she could gain some strength. Then she'd try again to get up and make her escape.

The wolf closed its eyes again. Unable to fight it any longer, Shannon rested her head against the tree and let the darkness overtake her.

* * * * *

Max woke to screaming pain rifling through his body. Every fucking thing hurt, from his head to his paws. But he was still strong enough to make it back to the house.

Shannon slept against the tree, her head tilted sideways, her face streaked with dirt, scratches marring the exposed skin of her arms and legs.

He laid there for a few minutes, admiring his woman. She'd been stupid to head into the woods to escape the wolves. If she'd stayed on the road she might have reached the store before they attacked.

Then again, maybe not. Savage bastards. It was going to take some effort to set them straight, but he'd mastered six of them at once. They knew now that there was a new alpha on the scene. One not to be fucked with. And he'd made sure to hurt them bad enough that they clearly understood to *never* get anywhere near his mate again.

He should have killed them. God, he'd wanted to after seeing the look of fear on Shannon's face, the scratches marring her skin, blood streaming down her arms.

Yeah, she'd been stupid all right, but damned brave, too. That's what made her perfect for him. One of the things he admired about her was her staunch refusal to give up in a fight. It made their battles more difficult, but then again when had he ever backed away from a good, rousing fight?

He knew it would always be that way between them. Theirs was a passionate bond, and passion sometimes meant fighting. He wouldn't want her any other way. If she'd been docile and agreeable, he'd never have chosen her for his mate.

To think he might have lost her tonight. His heart squeezed at the thought of never seeing her smile, never feeling her touch, never having her around to argue with.

Oh hell. He loved her!

His entire life he'd wondered what all the fuss was about when it came to love. His mother had smiled and told him when it happened, he'd know.

He sure as hell knew now. And dammit, it hurt. The need to protect her became more important now than ever before.

She could be carrying his child now for all he knew. And he'd let her slip away from him and almost get herself killed.

He'd teach her to protect herself better in the future. He'd train her in the ways of an alpha female. Maybe a trip to Boston to meet his family. His mother would set her straight, make sure she knew what being an alpha female meant. How she should demand the respect due her.

But first, he needed to get her back to the house. He shifted into human form despite the pain he knew he'd be in when his injures became human injuries. But they would heal soon enough.

Scooping an unconscious Shannon into his arms, he made the trek toward the house. It was only about a mile or so away. Not easy on bare human feet, but he'd manage.

Dawn would break soon, the soft gray light already filtering through the clouds that had hung low and black over the sky most of the night.

God, his body hurt. At least the bleeding had stopped, but the open gashes hurt like hell. Some of the bites had gone clear through to the bone, and his skin hung in shreds down his upper arms, shoulders and thighs.

Shannon, thankfully, only had minor wounds. Hers wouldn't heal like his, though. He'd have to treat them. Fortunately, she bore no marks from the other wolves. He would have had to kill any of them who touched her.

Finally, he reached the house and limped up the porch stairs, struggling to balance Shannon in his arms and open the back door.

After taking her upstairs and depositing her gently on his bed, he removed the remainder of her shredded clothing and inspected her body, noting that she at least had some color to her face. She wasn't pale, none of the scratches had gone too deep. She was bruised in spots, but none of her bones were broken.

He got out the first aid kit and cleaned her up, bandaging the wounds that needed it and washing her up with a soft cloth. He shuddered watching her nipples bead against the moist washcloth, his cock hardening instantly as he scented her musky perfume.

God. Beat up and bloody, barely able to move his body and he could still get a raging hard-on just looking at her.

His heart swelled with such unfamiliar emotions he could barely handle them. He pulled the sheet over her still-slumbering form and went into the bathroom, shaking his head at his reflection in the mirror.

Good thing Shannon was still unconscious. She'd be mortified if she could see him now. A human male with these kinds of injuries would be dead. Teeth marks had dug deeply into his shoulder, down both his arms, the wolves' claws having ripped away the skin on his back.

A horror flick couldn't do a better job of showcasing a victim of a wolf attack. He chuckled at that and stepped into the hot shower, wincing as the spray hit his open wounds.

Soon, they'd be gone. Restorative processes worked quickly on werewolves. It was just a matter of time, patience and gritting his teeth a lot. Then he'd be good as new.

Hopefully before Shannon woke.

* * * * *

The sound of running water stirred Shannon from her slumber. She burrowed deeper against the sheets of the warm bed.

Bed?

She sat up abruptly, realizing it was daylight and she was back in Max's bedroom.

But how? Had he found her out in the woods? And what about the wolf? Obviously she wasn't dead, so the wolf hadn't killed her. Nor had he hurt Max, who had to have been the one to rescue her.

She looked down at the bandages on her legs and arms, realizing that Max must have cleaned her up and tended to her wounds. Her heart swelled with the love she couldn't deny.

Maybe he was a hard-headed, dominating, overbearing dickhead at times, but she loved him. That in and of itself went a long way to making her think that it was possible they could work things out.

Slipping out of the bed, she stepped toward the bathroom. She heard the water turn off, meaning Max had finished his shower. Good. She desperately wanted to at least wash her hair. Maybe some plastic wrap around her bandages would do the trick. She was sore, still felt dirty from traipsing through the mud last night, and would love nothing more than to wash the grit from her body.

After that, she and Max could talk, see if they could come to some sort of agreement on how things were going to work between them.

Surely they could—

She gasped when she spotted Max standing naked outside the shower, a towel slung low over his hips. His back was turned to her and she put her hand over her mouth to stifle the scream she wanted to let out.

His body was destroyed. Angry, open wounds ravaged his body. Gashes so deep that bone was visible. Skin shredded so badly that he'd need grafting.

And it was everywhere. His torso, back and arms. How was he even standing? He needed to be in a hospital. She'd never seen wounds like that before on a man who was still alive, let along conscious.

"Oh my God, Max! What happened?"

He whipped around and his eyes widened. "You're awake."

His ribs were black and blue and bore the same open wounds as his back. She swallowed hard to fight back the nausea and rushed over to him, her arms outstretched. But she stopped, quickly crossing her arms over her chest, not knowing where she could possibly touch him. "What happened to you?"

He shrugged. "I'm fine. Trust me, these aren't as bad as they look."

Shaking her head, she followed him as he left the bathroom and headed into the bedroom. "Max, stop it! I don't understand. How can you be standing here, talking to me in a normal voice, when your body is nearly ripped to pieces? Please tell me what happened."

But she knew already. He'd come to save her, and the wolf had attacked him. Guilt settled in the pit of her stomach as she realized the havoc she'd created. He was hurt because of her, because instead of staying here last night and fighting it out with him, she'd run.

His hair fell in unruly black waves over his forehead. Quickly brushing it back with his hand, he said, "We have a lot to talk about. Give me a minute and we'll sit down and discuss this."

"Sit down and discuss? Are you insane? We need to get you to a hospital, now! Those wounds aren't going to heal on their own."

He offered her wry smile. "Yeah, they will. Watch."

Stripping the towel away, he stepped in front of the doorway leading to the balcony. Sunlight streamed through and shined on him. This was ridiculous. Was he hoping for a miracle? She was about to turn and run for the phone to call an ambulance when she noticed one of the wounds on his shoulder closing.

She blinked, certain she imagined what she'd just seen.

Dear God in heaven. He was healing right before her eyes. The wounds closed, the bruises disappeared, no scars were visible. In less than a minute, he was whole again.

"What the hell?" She flopped down on the bed, suddenly feeling very lightheaded.

"I can explain this." Grabbing for a pair of shorts, he stepped into them and sat next to her on the bed. She half-turned to face him.

"Explain what? How you healed? Maybe you should start with how you got those injuries in the first place. The wolf did it, didn't he? The one that sat by the tree with me last night. You showed up, he attacked you, right?"

"Not exactly."

"Okay, then tell me how exactly."

"I was attacked, but not by the wolf. By wolves. Six of them, to be exact."

The six that had attacked her. "How? When? Six wolves followed me into the woods. I ran and tried to get away but couldn't."

He smiled and nodded. "I know."

"And then this other wolf...what do you mean, you know?"

"I know what happened to you last night."

"How?"

"Some of it, I saw. The rest, they told me."

Maybe he had a fever. That had to explain his delusion that he could talk to wolves. "They told you."

"Yeah."

"How? Do you commune with wolves psychically?"

He arched a brow. "Sort of."

She reached out and laid her palm on his forehead, realizing her hand was shaking. "No fever."

Max laughed. "I'm fine, Shannon. Really. Now listen closely, because I have a lot to explain to you."

She'd try to sit still for his explanation. Then she'd call a doctor or take him to the ER. Whatever happened to him last night affected his brain. Although that didn't explain the devastating wounds healing as if by magic. This was all so confusing!

"Last night, you ran from a half-dozen wolves. You ran into a lone wolf who then fought with the other six."

Her pulse began to race. "How did you know that?"

He reached for her hand, his thumb gliding over her wrist. "Because I was there."

She searched his face, looking for a glassy-eyed stare, anything that would make this seem like some kind of dream. Maybe they were connected and he'd read her mind, pulled her memories. Hell, anything was possible.

"I don't understand. What do you mean you were there?"

"I'm surprised you haven't put it together yet."

"Put what together?" As soon as she said the words, something flashed in her mind. No, it couldn't be. Too farfetched. Too ridiculous.

"How could I be there to see it last night, Shannon? Search your heart. You know the answer; you're just refusing to see it."

How could she think straight when his thumb caressed the inside of her wrist, massaging her frenetic pulse? "I don't know what you're talking about."

"You were there, so were the six wolves. Who else?"

"Just the gray…" No. He was insane.

"The gray wolf? Yes. The one who approached you, then went around you to fight with the others. Do you know who the gray wolf is, Shannon?"

"No!" She wrenched her arm away from his grasp and stood, hugging her arms around her middle, refusing to put to words what ran through her mind. "That's not possible!"

He stood and approached her, reaching for her hands. She backed away and he dropped his hands at his side. "I'm surprised that you'd be so shocked, considering the magic you and your family possess."

She didn't want to believe what her mind told her was true, and yet the evidence stared her in the face. "You were outside my condo that night."

He nodded. "Yes. I followed you."

"Why?"

"Your scent called to me. I've wanted you as my mate from the first moment I saw your picture in a magazine."

She stared at him, open-mouthed. "What?"

His lips curled in a smile that made his face look boyish. How could this handsome man be the snarling wolf she'd seen last night?

"I felt a connection to you even then. After I met you, it became even stronger. I've come to Louisiana to set up my own pack, Shannon. I come from a very long line of Devlin wolves, and we're branching out. That's why I'm here. To start my own pack. I've already chosen my mate."

This was all too much to process. She didn't understand it, had more questions than she could possibly ask him at one time. "Mate?"

"Yes. Why do you think I wanted you to move in after last night? We're mated, Shannon. You're already mine. You can't escape that. It's your destiny."

Confusion turned to a burning anger. Anger that he didn't tell her what he was before he took her to bed. Rage at once again being told what was expected of her because of destiny.

She'd never let her family tell her what to do, and she'd sure as hell not be led around by Max.

"Listen to me very carefully, Max. I am not your destiny. I am no man's destiny. I make my own choices about what men I want to be with. You will never decide for me. My family won't decide for me. No one will decide for me."

"Shannon, I understand your—"

"You don't understand a damn thing! All you understand is what *you* want, when *you* want it and how *you* want it. You want me, but that's all I've ever heard from you. You've decided I'm your mate, that I should move in with you, but have you ever once asked what I want? No, you haven't. I'm sick of you and everyone else telling me what I should do and how I should feel!"

She knew she was nearly hysterical, but she couldn't help it. The last twenty-four hours had been too much to bear. She needed space, time and she needed to get the hell out of here and away from Max. Her feelings for him ran the gamut from gratitude that he saved her life at the risk of his own, to profound anger that he continued to tell her what to do.

He held out his hand to her. "Shannon, if you'll just let me explain…"

She backed away from his outstretched arm. "Don't touch me! I don't want to hear it, Max. The fact that you're this…this creature instead of a man…it sickens me. To think I had sex with an animal!!"

His face paled, his jaw clenched tight. He breathed in and out rapidly through his nose, and she knew he was holding his temper in check.

He was pissed. Good. She needed him to be, needed to strike out and hurt him to get him to back away, to quit giving her that sympathetic look that made her want to melt into his arms, to hold him close and never let go.

Because she finally realized that loving Max would mean giving up her soul, her very freedom. And that she wouldn't do.

Her heart wrenched at the hurt she saw in his eyes, but she steeled herself to ignore it. She had to. Self-preservation won out and she'd do whatever she had to do to get him to back off.

She marched into his closet and grabbed a pair of shorts and a T-shirt. Granted, they were way too large but she had no clothes to wear. "I'm calling my sister to come and get me. I'll wait downstairs. Do not come near me, and do not attempt to talk to me. I want nothing to do with you, Max. I'm disgusted by what you are, and I don't ever want to see you again."

Before she lost her nerve, before she looked into his eyes and once again saw the pain she knew she'd put there, she turned and hurried downstairs.

After calling Kaitlyn, grateful to realize the phones now worked, she stepped outside on the porch and paced. A hundred times she wanted to go back inside, fling herself into Max's arms and beg his forgiveness for hurting him, for lying to him.

But she couldn't do it. She had to stand firm. If loving him meant losing herself in the process, then it wasn't love. It would never work between them.

Knowing it didn't stop the tears from rolling down her cheeks, nor did it stem the anguish threatening to tear her up inside.

Kaitlyn pulled into the driveway and she hurried into the car, slamming it shut.

"Just drive," she said, noting Kaitlyn's concerned expression. "Don't ask, because I'm not going to tell you anything right now. I just want to go home."

As Kaitlyn nodded and drove away, Shannon had the feeling that she wasn't going home at all.

She'd just left home.

Chapter Thirteen

ઋ

Max paced the confines of the back porch, stepping up to the screen to look out over the water, then beginning his walk from one end to the other again. He felt caged, frustrated, desperate to take a run into the woods, but knowing it wouldn't help.

Shannon wouldn't take his calls, wouldn't see him, wouldn't speak to him. She hadn't shown up at work, and it wasn't like she was required to be there. The ad campaigns and press releases were finished. Now they just waited for the grand opening, so there really was nothing urgent that required her attention there.

How could he talk to her, to explain how he felt, if she wouldn't see him?

Alphas did not beg. It wasn't in his nature to lie down on his back and bare his vulnerable belly to anyone, especially a female.

Besides, Shannon had made it quite clear that she was disgusted with what he was. He sure hadn't counted on that reaction from her. Maybe he'd been too confident that she cared enough about him, wanted him enough, that it wouldn't matter what he was, especially in light of the fact that she possessed magic of her own.

So now what? What did an alpha werewolf do when he finds his mate, falls in love, but she doesn't return his feelings? It wasn't like he could go pick another. The thought of doing that left him empty. He'd already mated with Shannon. They were bonded. In a werewolf's world, that meant for life. His blood was inside her now. Hell, for that matter, his pup could be growing inside her, too. And he'd be damned if he'd allow her to raise his child without his presence. Or, God forbid, raise his child with another man.

Over his dead body.

Shit. He'd handled this whole thing badly. He should have told her about who he was before they made love, before they bonded. He should have waited to touch her, to taste her, until he was certain she'd accept him.

One helluva predicament.

His hearing picked up a car coming up the drive, his heart pounding at the thought that it might be Shannon. He stepped inside and went out the front door, disappointment racing through him as he saw Aidan step out.

"Hey there," Aidan said, waving an envelope in front of him. "Thought you might want to see the press releases that are going out next week."

Max had left the office early today, tired of wandering around aimlessly, unable to concentrate on work, and waiting to see if Shannon would show up. He pasted on a smile and said, "Thanks. Have time for a beer?"

Aidan bounded up the stairs and grinned. "Always have time for a beer."

After grabbing a couple bottles from the refrigerator, Max led Aidan out onto the back porch. They sat in the chairs and Max scanned the press release. "Looks good. I'd say we're ready to roll."

"Yeah, I think so too."

They both stared outside for a few minutes, drinking their beer in silence.

"You've got to give her a little time," Aidan finally said.

Max looked at him. "I don't think time is going to help much."

Aidan's mouth curved in a half-smile. "You'd be surprised. I know my sister. She's stubborn. Damned stubborn."

Max took a long swallow of his beer and nodded. "Don't I know it." It was one of the things he loved best about her.

"She also loves you."

Arching a brow, Max asked, "How do you know that?"

"We're connected. All of us. Not mind readers, but we can feel each other's emotions. She's miserable right now."

Great. Misery that he'd caused. That should endear him to her even more. "I never meant to hurt her."

"I know that. If I wasn't certain of that fact, I'd be here to kick your ass, not share a beer with you."

Max laughed, understanding that sentiment. He'd do the same thing if anyone hurt his sister. "So now what do I do?"

Aidan shrugged and finished his beer. "Wish I could tell you. I had enough trouble trying to figure out what to do about Lissa. I finally had to swallow my pride, smack myself upside the head and find her. I was going to tell her I loved her and keep telling her until she believed me."

"If only that would work in this case."

"All you can do is try. Granted, my relationship with Lissa isn't like yours with Shannon. You bring a little something 'extra' to the relationship that she'll have to deal with."

Max was taken aback. Did everyone know about him? "How did you know?"

Aidan grinned. "Mom told us the other day, after Kaitlyn explained that Shannon was a mess. She also warned us to stay out of it and let you two settle your differences by yourselves."

He made a note to thank Angelina for that. "Do you have any reservations about it?"

"Nah. If Shannon agrees to it and it doesn't hurt her, then what you two do and what powers you possess are your own business. I have enough of my own to deal with as it is," he said, winking.

"Thanks." Max shook Aidan's hand and walked him to the door.

"I hate to sound corny and all," Aidan said, "But you really have to dig deep and search your heart. You'll know what to do."

He nodded and watched as Aidan drove away, then went outside and walked to the edge of the water, staring into the murky depth as if they could provide the answer he sought.

Search his heart? He already knew what he wanted. He wanted Shannon. He loved her, needed her, and wanted her for his mate, by his side forever. But going to her and telling her that wouldn't convince her.

There was something else he had to do, and he knew what it was. It went against everything he stood for, his very genetic makeup. But if that's what he had to do to get her back, then he'd have to swallow his pride.

It was either that or lose her, and the concept was unfathomable.

He'd do it. It would kill him to make that sacrifice, but he'd do it for Shannon. He had to.

Tonight.

* * * * *

Shannon sat on the picnic table in the backyard of her parents' home. She drew her knees to her chest and rested her chin on them. Closing her eyes, she breathed in the crisp fall air, the slight breeze tinged with the sharp scent of earth's changing grounds.

Full-fledged change of season had finally come, cooling things off and leaving her with a melancholy feeling she hadn't been able to shake for days. Although she knew, at least partly, what caused her mood.

Max. She missed him. Desperately. Craved the sight of him, his touch, the husky tone of his voice and the smell of him, so like the cool, crisp earth she inhaled right now.

She'd argued with herself for days now, refusing to lend credence to what her heart was telling her. She couldn't go to him, couldn't become one with him. Not if it meant giving up her independence. She'd never be able to tolerate being dominated, being told what to do and when.

If they couldn't be equals, then they couldn't be together. And knowing what she did now about alpha wolves, she knew that Max would require control one hundred percent of the time. He would dominate her, make all the decisions, and she would have to follow along blindly. That she could not do.

"You gonna sit here all day and mope, or are you going to help serve?"

She looked up at the sound of Kaitlyn's voice, then slipped off the table and went inside.

Friday night dinner with the family. She hadn't wanted to come, but her mother told her in no uncertain terms she was expected to be there. She slipped into the kitchen and grabbed the salad and plates, making a quick turn and hoping she'd be able to sneak into the dining room before she was spotted.

"Shannon, wait."

No such luck. She halted and cringed at the sound of her mother's voice, knowing what was coming. Turning, she offered a carefree smile. "Yeah? Is there something else you'd like me to take in there?"

"No. Put those down and come sit with me."

With a forceful sigh, she handed off the bowl to Kaitlyn, who winked and headed into the dining room. Shannon followed her mother into the sitting room by the front window.

"Come sit beside me," her mother commanded, patting the sofa cushion.

Shannon sat and turned to face her mother, resolving to sit through the lecture and inevitable questions without offering any detail.

"What happened between you and Max?"

"I don't want to talk about it."

"That's what Kaitlyn tells me. You have to talk to someone about this, *ma belle*."

"No, I don't. There's nothing to say, Mom. It didn't work out."

"Did he hurt you?"

She had to smile at her mother's narrowed eyes, and she suddenly felt very loved and protected. "No, he didn't hurt me."

But she'd hurt him. Badly. He'd easily accepted her powers, the fact that she wasn't entirely human, without blinking an eye. Had she done the same for him?

No.

He'd risked his life to save hers, had taken on six wolves in a battle that could have easily killed him.

Had she thanked him for that?

No.

Then, he'd told her what he was, no doubt expecting the same acceptance of his unusual genetic makeup as he'd done for her. Had she accepted him?

"He's different, Mom," she said, pushing the guilt deep inside herself, praying that some day she might be able to forgive herself for hurting him.

"I know what he is, *petite*," she said, smoothing her hand over Shannon's hair.

She couldn't hide her wide-eyed stare. "You do?" When her mother nodded, Shannon shook her head. "You can't know. No one knows but me."

Her mother laughed. "I've known for a long time. Almost since he first arrived here."

"You know that he's a—" She stopped mid-sentence and looked around to be sure no one was within earshot, then finished in a whisper. "A werewolf?"

"Yes. I know that."

Shannon sat back on the sofa, unable to believe that her mother knew. "Does Dad know, too?"

"Everyone does, now. I told them the other day, after Kaitlyn said she had to come and get you. She sensed you were hurting. She also sensed your guilt."

Shannon didn't doubt that. It was difficult to mask remorse the size of the entire state. She turned her head to regard her mother. "So you all know."

"Yes."

"And you're okay with it."

Her mother shrugged. "It doesn't matter whether we're okay with it or not. None of us are in love with Max. You are."

She blew out a sigh and stared up at the ceiling, feeling more confused than ever. Sure, her family was fine with Max being a werewolf. Clearly they didn't understand what that entailed. For that matter, she didn't understand all of it. Other than the fact she'd have to give up control.

"You don't have to dominate every aspect of your life, Shannon," her mother said as if in answer to her thoughts. "Sometimes it's good to share, to give up a little control to the one you love. Not only does it take the burden off you, but it makes a relationship a true partnership."

"We could never have a true partnership. He'd want to be in control all the time. He'd want to dominate me all the time."

"Are you certain of this?"

"Yes."

Her mother took Shannon's hands and rubbed her fingers. "Don't be so certain you know. I have felt Max's heart. He has a deep love for you."

"Funny, he never told me that." She turned her head and looked at her mother. "Did he tell you?"

"No. He didn't have to. I'm not sure he even realized it at the time."

"He doesn't love me."

"Don't be so quick to decide how he feels. It's not your place to control his feelings. Maybe you need to step back a bit and give him another chance. You've always been quick to judge people, Shannon. Typically, your instincts are better than your outward logic. Let your heart decide on this."

Could her mother be right? Had she jumped to conclusions and just assumed Max would want to dominate her? Oh, she didn't know what to think anymore! Frankly, she was tired of thinking about it at all.

After dinner, she drove home alone. Kaitlyn was spending the night at the house so she and their mother could get an early start on shopping the next day.

Thankful to have the place to herself, Shannon took a shower and read for awhile, but couldn't concentrate. She tried to do some paperwork, but her mind kept drifting to Max.

She didn't want to think about Max. She didn't want to feel the guilt, the uncertainty, the intense longing that threatened to double her over.

Giving up, she slipped between the sheets of her bed and tried to sleep, but found she could only drift in and out, her dreams filled with a gray wolf with eyes of golden green. A wolf that stayed by her side, protected her, revered her, and transformed into a man who took her very breath away with his beauty.

She dreamed of Max crawling over her, whispering that he loved her, that he'd always take care of her. She felt the soft caress of his fingers over her bare skin. Her breath hitched as he slid his palms over her nipples, following the trail with his fiery hot tongue until she was writhing, begging him to—

She heard the growl on the fringes of her consciousness and sat up in bed, blinking her eyes, trying to adjust them to the darkness. Surely it had been part of her dream.

Then she heard it again, coming from the corner of her room. She looked over and saw the window was open, the sheer curtains billowing out in the cool breeze.

Shannon shivered and pulled the covers up to her chin, scooting away until her back hit the headboard. The growl grew closer. Yellow eyes glowed in the darkness as he approached the foot of her bed.

She shrieked in surprise when the wolf leaped onto the foot of her bed. He stared at her, not advancing, his watchful eyes waiting.

Waiting for what? For her to say something?

"Max?" she whispered, knowing full well it was him. Could he even answer her when he was in wolf form?

Obviously not. He didn't speak, didn't growl, just slowly crept up the bed toward her. When he reached her feet, he began to claw at the sheet, pulling it away from her until she was exposed. He sniffed at her feet, licking her toes. She fought back a giggle, still wary of his intentions.

She was more curious than afraid, knowing that he'd never hurt her.

"Your being here doesn't solve anything," she admonished, feeling stupid for talking to him. But surely he understood her.

He cocked his head to the side and looked at her as if he were intently listening.

She supposed he was giving her the opportunity to talk to him, without his being able to respond. She drew her knees up to her chest and wrapped her arms around them.

"Why are you here, Max? And why in wolf form? I've seen you like this before, so it's not a shock to me. Besides, you showing up here like this doesn't change anything between us."

He stood on all fours watching her, not moving.

This was her chance to tell him what was in her heart.

"I'm sorry I hurt you the other day. You don't disgust me at all. I fully accept what you are."

He leaned forward and licked her legs, rubbing his snout against her calf.

Tears filled her eyes at what might have been between them. Tentatively, she reached out and touched his head, loving the feel of his fur under her hands. She stroked his ears and he leaned against her, his long tongue licking at her palm.

She shuddered, wanting him naked here with her. In human form, their bodies entwined and making love. But that could never be. Not after what she'd done to him.

She hitched a breath and continued. "I can't be what you want me to be, Max. I can't be docile and let you control my entire life. It's not in my nature to give up control like that. Not all the time. Not the way you'd expect me to."

Then he did something that stunned her. He moved next to her and laid down, then rolled over, exposing his belly to her. Even the novice she was knew that was a sign of submission.

The alpha wolf of a pack would never show his belly to anyone.

But Max had just given her a sign. He gave up some of his control to her. He wasn't here to take, he was here to offer. And while she knew he'd never take a submissive role with her, she knew this to mean that he was willing to share equally with her.

Tears of joy streamed down her face. What it must have cost him to do this was incredible. She reached out and wrapped her arms around him, letting the tears fall freely onto his fur.

He stood and moved to the end of the bed. She watched in awe as his back legs elongated, his snout shrinking, his fur disappearing as he changed into a human again. The transformation took only a minute and yet was the most amazing thing she'd ever seen.

He smiled at her, a wary, tentative smile.

She opened her arms to him and he moved forward, dragging her against him and holding her tight to his chest. His lips met hers with the same fervor she felt. She poured out the pent-up anxiety and emotion she'd been holding in, wanting to show him how much he meant to her, needing to communicate her love for him. It was important that he knew, that he understood.

But before she could say the words, he dragged his mouth from hers and pulled back, his intense gaze searching her face. He caressed her cheek with the back of his hand and whispered, "I love you, Shannon. With my whole heart, my entire soul and every fiber of my being. I would be honored if you chose to spend your life with me. Become my wife, my partner, and stay by my side forever."

Her eyes filled with new tears and she nodded. "I love you, too, Max. I will gladly share all that I am with you."

Once again he took her mouth, slipping his tongue between her lips and coaxing a whimpered response as her body flamed to life. She felt the flow of her juices between her thighs as he caressed her neck, his fingers trailing lightly over her swollen breasts and belly until he palmed her sex.

"Open for me," he commanded.

She reveled in his dominance over her. This is where she would gladly let him take over. In this she would submit to him, the very act of doing so exciting her like never before. Spreading her legs, she allowed him access to her center, the part of her that pulsed and wept with need for him.

"Hurry Max, please," she begged, rewarded amply when he slipped two fingers inside her aching slit. His thumb drew lazy circles over her clit until she cried out with an orgasm held too long at bay.

But he didn't stop there. She had no more recovered her breath than he sat up and pulled her astride him, impaling her on his swollen cock. She gasped as he plunged in, his shaft reaching deeper and deeper inside her, until she could take no more of him. Then he reared back and thrust harder, his long shaft brushing against her sensitized clit until sparks shot through all corners of the room.

"Yes," he said, his tone triumphant. "Give me your magic, Shannon. All of it."

She did, wrapping her legs around him and sliding her buttocks back and forth, riding his cock as she'd dreamed of doing.

"Will you fuck me as a wolf?" she asked, barely able to form the words and yet wanting it more than anything.

"Yes, when I change you to one," he said through panting breaths. "If that's what you decide. You have to want it to make it happen."

A tiny spark of fear tightened her stomach, but she pushed it away. "I want whatever makes me yours, Max. In whatever way that is. I love you as a human, as a wolf, and I'll be by your side always."

After that they spoke no more. The night filled with harsh cries and howls of urgent passion as their bodies moved as one. She threaded her fingers through Max's thick hair and tugged hard. He responded by pummeling her with quick, hard thrusts of his cock.

Tears swept down her cheeks at the emotion he evoked within her. Her heart swelled with love for this man who was hers and hers alone.

"Mine," she whispered, sinking her teeth into the flesh of his shoulder as he had once done to her.

"Mine," he responded, sharp claws piercing the skin of her buttocks as he partially changed. She watched his green eyes grow more yellow, knew what was about to happen and welcomed it, knowing that she was his no matter what, and she would gladly accept her new status as Max's alpha female.

As her orgasm rushed through her and she felt the first driving spurts of his come shoot deep inside her, she felt herself begin to change, welcoming the burning pain along with the joy of her climax.

Tonight they'd run free together in the woods, the start of their new lives.

The Devlin dynasty of Louisiana had just begun.

Why an electronic book?

We live in the Information Age—an exciting time in the history of human civilization, in which technology rules supreme and continues to progress in leaps and bounds every minute of every day. For a multitude of reasons, more and more avid literary fans are opting to purchase e-books instead of paper books. The question from those not yet initiated into the world of electronic reading is simply: *Why?*

1. *Price.* An electronic title at Ellora's Cave Publishing and Cerridwen Press runs anywhere from 40% to 75% less than the cover price of the exact same title in paperback format. Why? Basic mathematics and cost. It is less expensive to publish an e-book (no paper and printing, no warehousing and shipping) than it is to publish a paperback, so the savings are passed along to the consumer.

2. *Space.* Running out of room in your house for your books? That is one worry you will never have with electronic books. For a low one-time cost, you can purchase a handheld device specifically designed for e-reading. Many e-readers have large, convenient screens for viewing. Better yet, hundreds of titles can be stored within your new library—on a single microchip. There a variety of e-readers from different manufacturers. You can also read e-books on your PC or laptop computer. (Please note that Ellora's Cave does not endorse any specific brands.

You can check our websites at www.ellorascave.com or www.cerridwenpress.com for information we make available to new consumers.)

3. *Mobility.* Because your new e-library consists of only a microchip within a small, easily transportable e-reader, your entire cache of books can be taken with you wherever you go.

4. *Personal Viewing Preferences.* Are the words you are currently reading too small? Too large? Too... ANNOYING? Paperback books cannot be modified according to personal preferences, but e-books can.

5. *Instant Gratification.* Is it the middle of the night and all the bookstores near you are closed? Are you tired of waiting days, sometimes weeks, for bookstores to ship the novels you bought? Ellora's Cave Publishing sells instantaneous downloads twenty-four hours a day, seven days a week, every day of the year. Our webstore is never closed. Our e-book delivery system is 100% automated, meaning your order is filled as soon as you pay for it.

Those are a few of the top reasons why electronic books are replacing paperbacks for many avid readers.

As always, Ellora's Cave and Cerridwen Press welcome your questions and comments. We invite you to email us at Comments@ellorascave.com or write to us directly at Ellora's Cave Publishing Inc., 1056 Home Avenue, Akron, OH 44310-3502.

erridwen, the Celtic Goddess of wisdom, was the muse who brought inspiration to story-tellers and those in the creative arts. Cerridwen Press encompasses the best and most innovative stories in all genres of today's fiction. Visit our site and discover the newest titles by talented authors who still get inspired - much like the ancient storytellers did, once upon a time.

CERRIDWEN PRESS

www.cerridwenpress.com